I0547976

STATIC

ORGONE

JAMIE GREFE

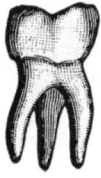

Bizarro Pulp Press
an imprint of JournalStone Publishing

Copyright © 2016 by Jamie Grefe

All rights reserved. No part of this book may be used or reproduced by any means, graphic, electronic, or mechanical, including photocopying, recording, taping or by any information storage retrieval system without the written permission of the publisher except in the case of brief quotations embodied in critical articles and reviews.

This is a work of fiction. All of the characters, names, incidents, organizations, and dialogue in this novel are either the products of the author's imagination or are used fictitiously.

Bizarro Pulp Press books may be ordered through booksellers or by contacting:

Bizarro Pulp Press, a JournalStone imprint
    www.BizarroPulpPress.com

The views expressed in this work are solely those of the authors and do not necessarily reflect the views of the publisher, and the publisher hereby disclaims any responsibility for them.

    ISBN: 978-1-945373-30-5

Printed in the United States of America
JournalStone rev. date: September 15, 2016

Cover Art: Matthew Revert
Interior Art: Luke Spooner
    www.carrionhouse.com
Interior Formatting: Lori Michelle
    www.theauthorsalley.com

STATIC

ALINA IS LOST in this tangled mess of gropes: cucumbered clefts, limbs and swells, white cotton stained and sopping, hard-yanked.

A hot sludge.

Sacs dangle like skin bells from strange men. Tonight, this desert house blurts soupy facials, spurts gaping waves of blue static through the walls.

Those among the debauched are the neighbors of the well-drawn shade. They are the colleagues of the creamed tonsil, of the velvet pelt and quivering hip.

Distant radiance of the nameless undressed.

Slip to a pink nipple, a wet lip skittering fluorescent in bath light.

Toes uncurl, a perfect row of red streaks. Cheek to tongue, a flap and lick, milk-jets on the bearskin.

Drinks spill down laps, bleed the shag sticky.

In another room, logs hiss, glow, and pop in the fireplace.

Everywhere, oiled bodies sparkle off dark corners. Liquid seducers. The lamped den shimmers, coating nudes in slick light.

Lek Gardenio smacks, gropes at a wall, oozes from a foggy bedroom to the hall and takes a breath to lean, careful not to drown under his own garbled spasm.

The unseen lurks.

From a side bedroom comes a whip-crack. Palm to posterior. Lek's balls still burn. His yellowed teeth clack, coated in muck. Amiss, he stammers forward, trying to stuff the lack with a scratch. There is no way out.

And his mustache of ferment.

And it makes his aching head burn solid jelly around this:

Private desert party—a place to ram holes in the doldrums.

A mistake, no doubt.

For there are too many floors to this maze of grunts. *Was it something I drank? Oh, what if it was?* he thinks. *The worm of a thought, perhaps?*

Hushed coos resound. "Lek, come, Lek," they say, with

lusty abandon. Or, "How about a hot mound and swig of gin?" they say. "If it's too hot—icebox your thermometer, old seadog."

But, who exactly mouths this summons for this shirtless, pantless, all but argyle-socked Lek, who stumbles in his near middle age to the pretzel bowl, to the fruit platter? He fumbles, itches across the room to the vegetable spread. Are his fingers crusty, joints weakened? Smothered and sweet sauced? He soaks a scrap of toast crust in a glob of bacon cream, crunches, trying to taste his way back to Alina, to his muse who has taken to mingling her fare elsewhere around the house, with some new body elsewhere around the house.

She left him hours ago.

Rewind to: a dip in the bottom of a healthy muff and Lek shot quick, obliterated. The shudder of a jackhammering index, a probing middle, a curious thumb skirting the rim of a fundament.

Now, wipe juice from nose.

It reeks of blood.

There are too many differences here, not to mention the static storms he suffers, threatening to crack open his skull.

Focus.

Alina is nowhere to be seen in this mess of moaning holes. But Lek thinks, *Yes, I do believe I recognize you, I know you from our mutual acquaintances, I think I've seen your faces*: Wade's goo-smothered shaft, his face screaming, "Slurp mine honey." Or, Sandy sliding legs open, oiling some buff goon's chicken bone, and popping it out on purpose, going to work on it with hairy tongue flicks.

Lek fingers a stale pretzel.

There, by the stereo, a reverse expulsion, a peony stuffed, plunged. He bites, saltier. There is a hum in the room, a reverberating whistle.

Plunge.

Into the throes of—the bacon cream, the skinned shrimp, salad dressings, red plastic cups.

And then she—the anomaly—happens.

Out of the steam of a side door, a young brunette in black-rimmed spectacles, painted-on jeans, and cardigan green approaches. She grabs Lek's hand—he's taken to wiping cream-streaks on his thigh—guides him toward her.

Behind her, someone says, "Full sleaze ahead," and rushing from out of frame to focal point, a curly-haired Absalom propels himself over the leather sofa and plops awkward in the lap of a stuffed limb sandwich, the living room somehow wider now, looming open now.

The brunette tugs him off to get his attention. He says, "I really can't—Alina, my lover is—I don't know about this—*ooogaaalllooogaaa.*"

"You're with me now," she says. "I'm your only hope."

"She's all over the bathroom, son," some hunk slurs from across the room. ""Don't let that diamond in the dark slip you up." This man bumbles across the room, perhaps, to speak more frankly with Lek and the brunette, but he cannot be sure, for the brunette, with Lek in tow, tugs him away.

"This is not the end of the line," she says over her shoulder, more to the odd man than to Lek. "A painless resolution remains."

Lek pulls a corner of his own mustache into his mouth, trying to keep himself in check. "Surely," he says, "this is a confusion of who you think I am."

"But," the brunette says, "it's not just lust, Gardenio." She giggles, bending her middle finger inward to tickle Lek's palm. "You'll learn to ignore those impulses if you only listen." And they continue off through the brambles of skin and house, of teeth, veins, thighs, feet.

The gurgling of the house has grown louder. More bodies Lek has not seen in his life. *If I dart away*, he thinks, *just to make it to the coat rack, or what if Alina is already back at the car?* But the brunette squeezes his hand too tightly. *Alina*, he thinks, *my light in the shadow of this dumb show. Why, my dear, how have we arrived here?*

His mind skips, jumps to Alina at the office picnic in the city park, her black skirt mustard-smudged like a smeared yolk on black canvas. That was buns and buns ago. Some wiener antic he can't properly remember—and even if he could? The question startles him. And there he is again dropping the stapler on her sandals. And how minutes later (perhaps hours, he can't focus) he clinked coffee mugs with Alina at the microwave in the break room. She had told him the toaster stunk as if scorched, pointed out an old flier on the bulletin board. He only heard her accent, smelled the buttons on her blouse.

He says, "Can you tell where we . . . ?" But this brunette does not speak, just pulls and leads. Pass door upon grumbling door: sweat and musk and armpit stink.

A shape creeps closer. His boss, Briggs, the bald oaf, waves his arms as if he has a deal to seal with the air itself. But two blonde twins, giggling, shoot out of the dark, pirouette before the boss, halt him obscenely with their tied tongues. One of them cups his pickle, slaps his buttocks to a jiggling tango.

The hallway pulses dark green from little circular lights in the ceiling. Lek's whisked away under them. And under him the carpet feels warm growing warmer.

The voice of an old man booms from behind: "She'll cut you, son. Wouldn't be the first time in this tollbooth of deception."

Whatever that means, thinks Lek. But he's distracted by spice, the remembered plume of Alina's peachy hair. Her neckline in the morning, a vase. Tiny leg-lines where the prickly hair spots poked skin. Pretty sprinkles of pepper.

"Don't look at any of them now," his brunette seducer says sharply, not looking back, charging on. "It's what they're here for."

"Where *are* you taking me?" Lek says. "I should be getting my coat," But he slips on a trail of rubbers on the floor. She yanks. He pushes on, feels the goop dribble out.

"Lek," someone from the kitchen yells, "welcome to what lies between." And how many steps have they taken? How long is this hall? Is it shriveling to a paste? But is it shriveling at all, not glitching to a blurred row of blue doors?

Lek passes the kitchen. It's Georgette, the mechanic who flushed the transmission on his convertible just last week. She's being serviced, bent over a faux wooden island in the center of a kitchen so big it could house a dock. She cleaves at mutton, hair spilling over her face, gives Lek a toothy grin, bob, nod, shiver, shudder.

STATIC

"I can't very well—" Lek says. "Hey—have you seen Alina?"

"—time for a pole-sniffer like you," Georgette mouths, rammed hard by her suitor who accelerates and pops, spoons a clump of cream pie all over her tattooed back.

Lek is hand-squeezed down the never-ending hall. He passes barreling bodies of skin. Some nod, stare, clap.

An open door.

Footsteps stomp above, muffled.

And Lek has given up questioning his destination, assuming it to be some kind of Moroccan themed hash bar tucked in a hidden closet or a chest of drawers stuffed with socks. Of course, where he last left Alina—was she relieving herself in the bathroom to a crowd of limp sailors?—and how to snag her attention long enough to get her to leave is the coin of his dilemma.

And this is when, abruptly stopping in front of the last door on the left, the last door before the stairwell rises to meet the upper reaches of the house, he sees her.

Lek gives a vicious yank to shake off his seducer's grip.

It looks like her, but a hair taller, her edges not crisp, blurred in a jittery frame. She's coming undone. She's gorgeous, oblivious. He rubs his eyes.

"It can't be . . . " he says.

The room before him is a sterile motel vignette, shitty windows opening to a fog-soaked nightscape.

Lek doesn't recall seeing this room during his jaunts through the house, through the plugging of licked holes. *How can this be here?*

He reaches out an arm, rims his lips, and continues to soak up the strange room before him as if his outstretched hand could somehow flick away this motel replica of Alina.

The wood-paneled television tuned to static.

The dark green bedspread and starched pillows, head-dented.

Alina stubs out a cigarette—she's clad in a white towel—stands, and wrenches the window open to let in a square sheet of black fog.

A man's hands reach inside, quickly grip and grab Alina under the arms, towel and all, and scoop her sweetness out into the foggy void.

And that man leans forward.

What Lek sees is a man with a plain thin gaunt ugly September face, eyes quaked in shadow, and a dead-grass scrawl of stubble atop his lip. And, finally, on top of the man's plain thin gaunt ugly September face rests a cowboy hat the color of weathervane rust. Lek reads that face, "So long, farewell—give up, fair night—She's mine," as if spoken in a voice already on the inside of his mind.

And the man vanishes.

Lek is about to burst, his argyle-clad calves already poised to propel his spent self across the room and out the window, but the brunette (ever carefully) finger-wraps (for the second time) his rod and twists it up like knobbing an oiled nub. His nose holes pulse, heat up. *Where is that man taking Alina? And what is the meaning of this vision if that is, truly, what it is? Is this delirium? Did someone slip something wanton into the punch: a crushed pill, love juice, a shot of dread?*

He wants to throw up, throw a fist through the walls of this house. Seed spread across the bellies of too many unknown faces of this night, Lek sucks air to push away his weakness. "How is this . . . ? The hell did she go?" he says to the empty room. "There's something wrong with this goddamned house."

His forehead clenches, lines squiggling, aching, noise whirring inside his skull.

The brunette tugs lovingly as if medicating him. She won't let him go. A soft pulse in her grip. A clenching keeping him near. It's all too much. His nose is plugged.

Lek finger-flicks the air, scatters dust and flies. If this were only a game played with the rub of a thumb, the mashing of buttons. This cannot be shut down. Something strange cut and drawn or uncut—the wholly singular, unbound and explicit: a lament, the vignettes, the priest, smoke, metal snips snipping flesh.

"That's my crotch of—ow!" he says to the woman. "Enough, you're rubbing me sore."

The brunette places one hand on Lek's chest, says, "She wants you to follow fairies down fairy holes." Her voice is soft, urgent. "You never knew better and we have no time to waste, Gardenio. This is beyond what *you* want." She pauses. "I'm sorry."

STATIC

Lek inhales: shrimp, horseradish sauce, semen, cinnamon. And the sounds from this hallucinatory house well up with Janet and Pete, Wade and Cynthia, Bob and Bob, Jessica and Rob, Roy and Georgette. And more. The moans rush the hall in pulses of light.

The room before them has twisted back to normal, just a bed of filth.

"Step up, step up the stairs," the brunette says. "It's a way for you to save yourself, Lek. Trust me."

And for the first time all night, Lek really looks down at his naked body. Only socks. Socks and the rank of his own skunk-sweat.

The brunette nuzzles her face into his neck. She says, "This house is not a crypt, it's the birth of choice." She spins, goes behind Lek and slaps his ass hard. He stammers, but steps.

And behind Lek, the orgy melts into a frenzy of mashed limbs. The players are sticking and jamming and ramming their goods around teeth and tongue, deep up into clefts, chewing calluses and scabs. Someone's turned the stereo to pure static.

Lek moves painfully up the stairs.

Toward the letting go.

But Alina has not been whisked away by a mustachioed man in a dreadful hat. No, she is in one of the house's many regal bathrooms, rolled in a shower of legs, fruit-flavored soap, slippery torsos, lips and tongue-tips.

Here, in this shower, women and men crush up against Alina. Her breaths come quick. She throws her beautiful head back and cackles.

A hairy arm slides out and up from between a pair of thick legs. Blonde hair mashes against Alina's mouth. Her tongue, coated in blonde fur. She spits, angles her head around to take a breath of something other than hair and steam. The arm reaches. Fingers poke up from behind. The steam rises, too thick to see past.

The toilet flushes, gushes gallons of water.

"Are you waiting for him to return?" a voice says, near her ear.

Who? But the hand works a jig around her pouch. She cannot move in this sloppy skin. More soap slithers across her back like bubbles drizzling down her crack.

Alina shivers, feels her body grow thinner as if more women are throwing themselves into the shower, pressing her deeper into this cream chamber. "I have seen him with a chestnut angel of deception," the voice says. "How does that make you feel? Does it make you feel a hundred fingers inside you fading to Hell?"

The man's fingers dig up inside her.

And the bodies crush her lungs, her chest, her ancient bones. That hairy arm suddenly wraps round her neck. It does not squeeze. Still, she cannot breathe right. A blackness crackles, sparkles behind her eyes. A darkness and the arm's constriction is a reminder of how far she's come and under these conditions of extreme pleasure of what it means to experience the chance of entrapment.

Alina shudders, excretes an orgasm. It tips her body to hum, shiver. Her body is too pushed to other wet bodies. They rattle, squeak. Yet, her coming causes the coming of others around her as if they can feel from within. And her skin drips orgasmic.

Women squeal like piglets.

Men huff like boars, snort gravel.

The man behind her, the one with his arm around her, says, "When I was child and all that, I had a pillow—night friend softness—with a scissored hole. Led down into the meat of the mattress vortex. It grinds a member to nothing but sick, sick, sick hope."

Alina's eyes roll up into her head. She's feverish chills, fire, a lamb. She can't stop coming syrup-waves out her skin. "Who?" Alina speaks, her mouth moaning steam, sludging out the words. The man's fingers unceasing, his arm tightens around her throat. "Did you imagine a God made of sweat stains?"

The explosion from her snatch is a clumping drip that oozes between toes.

The shower burps and the hot juice rises in this sealed box of suffocation. The shower door buckles, expands to meet the pressure of all these bodies. The secretions and gasps of so many pig-people.

But the door holds, fills, buckles.

Water rises, turns the shower to a bath of ooze. A fury of release. "Oh, Lek," she cries out, the orgiastic sweetness filling her mouth, coating her teeth. "I kept all this so far away and now your tables have turned to chopping blocks of sacrifice—I'm going to kill you." But she does not speak these words, cannot speak with musk-soaked lungs in this mess of limbs and fingers and it's as if the man fingers the valves of her heart. "I must remain."

The water bleeds red. The blood of her heart singing shudders to burst. And the hole between her legs tugs far enough open for the man to crawl up into her, just inviting enough for him to pull the insides of her out.

And let truth spill to death.

And she smiles for what will be.

Up the shag stairs. Lek's naked arms flail, fingernail the wall and his messy argyles slump step to sliding step.

He snorts. His knees buckle under the pressure of an unknown weight, a sack of dirt. But all the dead leaves of Lek's mind have burned to skin, veins and static. In the nightlight of the dashboard, Alina had stroked his leg, scissor-stroked his crotch, and told him, "We need a signal, something we can do with our fingers so we know when we should leave if it's all too much."

His vision blurs shag. Sweat drips down his nose. But the shag is not made of sheepskin or tumbleweed. "There is no priest here, no fatherly guilt," is a thought Lek holds. "I was raised to be better than lust," he says aloud.

Take another step.

But the stairs have twisted to an almost flat field of crust. Just bumps like tiny breasts made of yellow and black gum. Lek is slanted at an angle and he suddenly touches his cock as if using it as a night-beacon to guide him forward in the fuzz. The music of his trumpet hums a jig that seems to say, "Keep walking and step, one, two, step, one, two."

There must be an end to these stairs.

Alina must be up there somewhere.

STATIC

Don't slip.

And Lek slips.

His argyles fly airborne. He reaches out for further stairs to grasp. He must pull himself to the apex, to the mountaintop, to the pinnacle. His cock rugburns on the shag. The prickles of palm trees and the memory of sunlight obscure his fantasy of Alina, light of his stubborn wounded heart. And pull, Lek, a voice chants. To the top. He does.

Lek does. He's a marching drum.

Feel gums mash powder to cream bits.

Cock spark-dragging the shag, keep going, Lek.

Ignore possibility and if you slip, you will never, ever make your way to that grave in the den of lions where sweet Alina prepares to pounce.

The Palm Desert's Highway Motel.

Night.

A neon sign glitches pink in the puddled reflection of the highway. A sixteen wheeler roars past.

A car door slams shut. The parking lot hums dust.

A man's hand reaches down, tugs argyle up his calf, heads straight toward the row of pink doors. Those doors line the facade. But there, nestled between two particularly shimmering pink doors, stands a woman who looks like Alina.

She hits a cigarette. She's wearing a cardigan to compliment our approaching man's frumpy suit. Her bobby shoes sparkle sugared noir in the moonlight: lips curl a wicked grin, eyebrows penciled sunset pink, arched, and her nose wiggles. She takes another drag of smoke and blows a gentle storm of stink toward the man.

"Did you enter him, baby?" she says. "Done deal?"

"The devil don't feast on bread alone, does he?"

"Castrated and bleating is what I hear."

"Or in socks that stink," the man says. And he's pressing his dirty suit into her breasts. She lets flow a fog of smoke into his eager mouth, shotgunning a stream of tar into his lungs. He takes it. He accepts it.

And, yes, the man's other hand reaches around to guide Alina ever closer to the grime he wears on his skin. This man of dirty fingers, this man with the face of blurred grime, kisses the woman like grinding iron to melt. A crackling weld in their kiss. Alina pushes her needy lips to his lips and releases, runs tongue across cheek.

"Told you, baby," she says, "said, baby, this is how it all goes down. Love's a stuffed pig, overblown, swag-swallowed by the thought of tail. Must have hit the jackpot."

"You'll have him."

"Can't wait to trim him," she says. "Means three humdingers for you, sailorman."

The man's hand touches her cheek, shakes. Alina takes his hand. He pulls away, says, "Now I see these hands as slabs of meat."

"For *my* abattoir," Alina says. "Meat's death, until you cook it."

The door behind the woman opens as if on its own. Somehow, in the opening of the door, there is now a cowboy hat on the man's head, glitching, appearing and disappearing with a will of its own.

They enter the doorway, into the glow of a black and white television in the corner. It lights the room in monochromatic stutters.

Green shag carpet and the man's boots, muddied. Alina sits on the bed. She watches. The television plays an old film wherein a woman stands waving her trench-coat-clad arms frantic in the middle of a desert road. Headlights illumine her body. An old sports car slams on its brakes, nearly crashing into her. It's a man in a suit who is driving the car. The two talk in quick arm flails and exaggerated mouths. The scene on the television repeats, slows to heavy frames per second, repeats slower, until it stops.

The motel man crosses to the bathroom. He avoids touching the bed, Alina's legs spreading so subtle. He avoids the small end table and the wooden chair. He does not take notice of the black telephone or the bottle of J&B. He shuts the bathroom door.

A telephone rings.

The ring is muffled, or perhaps, it's the man's dirty ears. The phone rings through the piss the man drizzles around the toilet rim. One hand grips dick. One hand flexes, splits up in static, fleshes. And when he steps from the bathroom, he feels a house of limbs smothered in a blasting ocean of saxophonic drone. He feels the sudden impulse to answer the phone, for he doesn't know how he knows, but he knows the phone is for him to answer.

Alina appears transfixed by the television scene, entranced: halted woman, mouth agape, dead, just still.

The man lingers over his own hand. His hand breaks up again in static, sizzles, melts to noise. He reaches out, arm held before him. Suddenly, can't move through the electric muck of the room.

Alina is no longer there.

The man floats slowly as if pushed to the phone. Don't tell him he's lost his clothes. He reaches down to pick up the phone. And his hand of static trembles over the receiver. The phone stops, the rings are silenced.

And the man halts in the beams of his own confusion.

A gutted lamb.

Elsewhere, the foggy door to the shower cracks, sends naked women and heaps of men a-tumbling to the floor in a tangle of limbs. They roll ass over throat, a pile of skin on the tiled floor, slippery, slopping fish.

A mustache jams ribs on the toilet. A blonde smacks skull on sink. Alina's legs are cocooned into a flabby gut-wound. She clenches lips, twists something fluffy. More flaccid tentacles rain around her. The steam makes it hard to see.

Alina's on her back, overcome by the pulse of the room's light. It smothers her with limbs and licks, just as the rest of the bathers tornado from the shower.

A stifled moan, high-pitched.

A woman's neck caught on the rim of the shitter, sliced open on a shard of glass.

Blood spurting across skin.

And Alina can't be sure if she should miss Lek or merely miss the thought of him—like that could be possible. And the floor of the bathroom—the wet, the vile, the bile—writhes with licked pelts, stroked rods, and slurped skin-straws.

She is smothered by the shadow of a nipple.

The man hovering over her, a grey haired wildcat, licks around her mountains, greedy. He smears gelato—is he fingering a cone?—on her navel and flicks cream, double-dips, and skitters. His tongue slides down to her love tuft. Alina's teeth grind. She spits water. She spits up shampoo. *I can't miss you now, Lek. You're not wanted here. I can't imagine how I should miss you now.*

Of course, she had met Lek in the office. The paper and ink, the bandwidth and the sore ass from the hard bottom of a squeaky chair.

The night shift bled to morning.

Alina's blouse stained brown (just a splotch) and how Lek had dabbed at her breast stain with a wad of wet paper towels on a wind-torn night.

She recalls his anecdotal television, some soundless loop, buffering, stuttering on, off. Yes, there was a video playing. It was the video of a woman standing in the middle of a desert road, blinded by headlights.

Now, Alina, legs bent to chin, endures this grey man licking and sucking. He smacks his lips, holds her ankles, and she's confused. Shouldn't be, but so it is.

And here is only heaps of slashed limbs and testicles, breasts and tummies. They pump like androids, like parasites, like maggots.

Hairs tickle her ear. Another woman has come close in the confusion. And Alina hears water.

The shower must still be running. It smells of marbled meat.

A toilet gurgles.

A telephone—muffled.

Her signal.

The heat of this overflowing bathroom is starting to stifle.

This is when the floor drops. It's been drooping the entire time. The orgy itself has fleshed it to hold. And the rumble. And the ring. The ring wells deep in her lower belly. A tongue flicking candle wax on the back of a stripper. A tongue lapping come puddles. She shudders. Everything churns closer and closer.

STATÎC

Lek is sopping wet, suddenly drenched. The wet turns his socks to galoshes, the shag carpet is a river of argyle soft as skin.

He's still in the house.

The second floor.

There is a telephone on the bed stand of the bedroom where he finds himself panting. He lunges to answer it, trips over the bed. His body flops sideways, legs akimbo over his head. And his arm reaches out for the ring, cradles nothing.

Mid-ring of the seventh ring: "Hello?"

"Hello?"

"Alina is this—?"

"No."

"Who then?"

"You remember your friend, don't you, Gardenio? Your always friend?"

"Wrong person," Lek says. "You shouldn't be—you can't, I mean—"

"This is your always friend. You remember your friend, don't you?"

"Is this some kind of prank, you prick?" Lek says, itching crud off his droop. His eyes flit around the room, out the window. He's looking for his car in the driveway, but he cannot see his car in the driveway. The desert dark is too thick, too many flies crowd the glass.

"You drove," the voice says. "I am here, too. Alina and I, too, Lek. You remember your always friend, don't you?"

"Come and get me then," Lek says, his voice breaking into a hiss. "I need to speak with Alina. Put her on."

A sudden yelp blurts the line. It's a yelp Lek has heard before, the throaty moan of a lover in throes.

Of ecstasy.

And the sound of crunched glass.

"All broken in the bathroom," the voice says. "Come see your always friend." And the voice is too clear, too close. Static oozes from the receiver. Lek screams, lets the receiver go, hears a buzz, drops the phone.

21

An unzipping. His brunette escort who abandoned him at the base of the stairs has, unbeknownst to Lek, made her way onto the bed. She eases off her glasses, her jeans. The room is bleached red. Moans roar through the window. She breathes jazz strokes in the way she dips her full body to will his cock to stand. It's a suggestion, a question, a provocation.

Their mouths melt into the parting of legs, a pair of black handled scissors on the bedside table. Between lip to lip, Lek says of Alina, "How will you ever forgive me?"

But his escort's scent of intoxication pummels him. She guides him within the abyss.

Lek says, "I cannot hide within an ache."

He shuts his eyes, prostate gushes spunk to quell the fever. His spine drips.

Lek swallows.

The escort leaves clothed, wordless, and he's left with streaks of seed pooling on the bed.

And Lek pants, slides off the bed in a slither, under the bed to a spot in the under-dark, where, if he wills his way further, might sink into the skin of the house.

He slides the black-handled scissors into his grip, clicks them thrice.

Night shadows from outside dim the room like a cloak.

Lek's fingers shiver, grip the carpet before him, hold the scissors, and pull his body to the doorway. *I've failed.*

Later, Alina's eyes gape at the spanking blows by a bearded man, devil horns propped on his mop of curls. He's laughing wildly, slapping at her bum in upward strokes. She's bent over his knee, a fleshy mannequin: resolved, made anew.

This is the living room, a mass of humping bodies, the light, a swirl of blue orgone. Someone has let a smoke machine shoot candy-flavored smoke to blow waves, to suck.

A skin-sword plunges Alina's mouth. She takes it.

All darkens quickly.

But Alina hasn't always been here. And the gross dick quells the confusion of where Lek has run off to and how he will return—soon, his time will come.

STATIC

Devil-horns fingers her petals, operas a tune in Italian and he thrusts harder. She grunts, presses back onto his finger. She shuts her eyes to not think pithy. Her mouth is emptied, shots dribble over her tongue. It's a feast. She hears choirs upon choirs dissolve. It could be the air conditioner. It could be the palm trees slapping the windows. And why are the windows boarded up with bent-back nails? The smell of rusty skin rotting. The smell of her own body.

The entire room is a symphony of sex sounds grown orchestral.

But the guests are crowding more violently. Bodies stuck together. Sex toys scatter and flop. There is an intensity in the room, an intensity Alina's mind is shoving aside in favor of skin rammed between her teeth.

If only she could escape is the thought she wants Lek to think.

The hummed pleasure, the breathed pleasure, the overall manifestation of pleasure in the room, though, is shifting unsteady. More rush closer. The smell of blood. The smell of a ripped open body.

He's near.

Outside, miles away.

The man palms desert dirt, clenches, and clumps it to the wind for the vultures to spit. They circle unseen, yet heard: the beating of wings, beaks click, slavering for skin, wet blinking chews.

And this man walks the mountain road. He's miles from the metropolis, so many lights pepper the horizon far below— towering buildings, expressways, city drone. And the man hums old noise to himself, stuffed full of orgone squawks. His lips buzz out a trumpet. Fingers hiss, snap, click.

Hiss. Snap. Click.

He waits for another car to come up the road. He moves forth in the dust. So many have passed thus far, all on their doomed way to the sliced finale.

It is only correct to construct semblance for a mad-show such as this one.

STATIC

Stop.

Don't move.

It is not the wind, this grind. This snarl. This tearing open. No, it is the sound of squealing tires echoing up the mountain.

And instead of obeying the wind of the road, he runs wild, crosses the mesa like a coyote.

"Will you be coming around the mountain, son?" he says, chest heaving, legs in acceleration.

The mesa dips to a curved dent off the road where he finds—

An upturned automobile.

On fire.

The other car still approaching.

"Believe, son," he says. "Smother yourself in it."

Or a tall office building in the metropolis speckled with tiny lights.

"Often work late, not this late?" Lek says, thumbing his nostril. "Lately biting at the reigns—all from a damn phone call, huh." He straightens his tie, the knot lopsided around an unbuttoned collar. A goofy trout pattern in the light of the office hall. Ink stains on the carpet.

"Overtime," Alina says. "Loyalty's sucked up more hours than an armadillo at an ant parade." She's walking past to the break room, swivels, turns at the copy door, enters quick.

"For Briggs, that old bear?" Lek says, raising his voice toward the copy room. And the beat of silence calls Lek to limp faster, to grip mug and follow. "Was it Pete gave you all this jazz?" he says.

"Or Wade," Alina says. And a hum-click-hum of a corner copier ghosting blank paper from its smooth jaws.

"One of those bozos, huh," Lek says. "Cracking the proverbial workplace whip."

Alina lifts a thick lid, looks, licks her lips, lowers it, places pages face down in the tray, taps them neat. "Just dreaming of fun," she says.

"Fun's good," Lek says, elevating his eyebrows.

The copier spits the paper out halfway, hauls it back up inside, flips and squirts, and slips page upon page out double-sided, full of ink.

Lek leans against the doorframe, face shadowed by the dim hall. A comforting hum.

"Wearing your grin lopsided or is that a frown I detect?" Alina says.

"Tired Fridays, this duty drags," Lek says. "Did I tell you I had this dream about you the other night? In the rain." He steps into the copy room's glow. He sips too-thick instant coffee, watches the paper stack and spit, click and snap. "Too bright to tell the truth, too many people. I was inside some kind of motel room—you have certain dreams, but your mind wants stone walls, so you get wood walls instead, yeah? Could be you're standing outside on someone's giant mountain of shit-shingles, bones for chandeliers, whatever, but you were somewhere there, Alina, and I had to find you—wasn't pretty."

"And then you woke up weird?" Alina says. She's stapling small stacks of blackened white together. The pile maker. The dream listener. The corner stapler.

"Woke flat—don't know if I woke or rolled off the bed." Lek sets down his cup on the same table Alina uses to staple those stacks of paper, piling them into three stacks.

The cold night air struggles, whips at the window in whistles. Lek presses his back against the wall, keeps the window to his side. It makes him look small there by the window.

He feels tall.

"Night dreams abound for you, huh," Alina says, stapling hard. "A struggle to get up."

"Another woman in the dream, two women, maybe more than two, I thought was—don't take this in the wrong light—you, all of them like Alina was their name. I don't know how I can say it."

She doesn't reply.

Wet palms. Lek's been staring at the way Alina stacks the papers. A city of small crosses. Reams of paper form white stacks, the backsides of whatever work they are to mean. "It was—just nothing."

"Sounds, yeah?" Alina says. She's just standing there now, standing like Lek was standing before he moved to the window, moved to the side of the window, hovering in this in-between time of their talk.

STATIC

He hunches forward to the table, slides his cup across, to the paper cutter, holds the cup by its semi-circular handle, light hitting the grey-blended paint.

"Another one of your Nyquilian nights, Lector?"

"I slept early that night, I think," he says. "It's Lek, just call me Lek."

She nods. "Talk later. I'll be up on the forty-third—the dreaded top-corner cubicle for the next two hours. Will you—you should drop in, dream weaver."

Lek positions himself to the side, back now to the window, perfectly framed in that window. Eyes on the mug, the mug by the paper cutter. He touches his nose. It's wet around the rim. Index and thumb rung-round in nostril-sized dollops of blood, dimes on his tips, blood on his swirls.

Take the cup.

Pick it up.

Alina's gone.

Lek limp-sprints, looks out into the hall, but the hall is not the hall of this company, instead, it is a window looking into a motel room facing the bed.

He dares not take another step, can't step.

Alina, white-toweled, sits on the bed.

Lek stumbles to the side, grips the wall, looks away from the scene. His legs jiggle, buckle, and his garbled grunt is a static blast, a wall of noise. *Swallow, keep it here*, he thinks. This shudder. *And what would happen if the world cracked? What would happen?* Lek's nose plugs, sputters yet more blood. He stumbles back, bends over, one arm outstretched, fingertips on the copier to hold him up.

The door is a passage.

The door cannot be.

And from down the hall, Lek hears the sound of several telephones ringing, the rings crescendo to a shrill drone. Lek zombies away from the door. His head cracks up, though, to catch one more sight of the motel.

All of a sudden, blood rivers out his nose.

He drops to his knees, crumples a cowboy hat he's been holding the whole time, slips, hits the floor. He looks up at the ceiling of stars, pulls the hat out from under him.

He snorts the welling blood up into his skull, stands and spits. Darker now, more blood on the floor now.

But another voice is trying to break through, it's the voice of the copy room. "Don't do it," he says to himself. "Don't go there.How many times do I have to tell you not to go there?"

"Shut yourself up," Lek says. "I don't listen to you."

"What if there are others like this? Like this, Lek? Like this?"

The stirring fizzle inside Lek rises. He tips the cowboy hat into place, just to darken the room, cool his burning eyes. He puts one finger on one nostril and forces out a gob of snot and blood. He clears his throat, tries not to listen to that other voice. The woman on the bed is too beautiful for voices, for his voice. For his entire life.

Lek limps back to the copy room window, down at the dark.

Behind him, the doorway is coated in static, but the woman on the bed is still there.

He turns to face the door, crouches. He's a limp bull and charges, more monster now than man.

To become the man he—

Static hands turn real as meat in the frozen television light of the motel room. The man moves to the bed, touches the messy bedspread. Sheets steam warm with the lingering aura of a body. She was here and this man's rough hands tear the blanket from the bed, cast it to the green shag carpet floor.

Damp stains on the spread.

On the television, a woman's frozen mouth gapes, spread wide in white and black. A film the man has seen before, but can't place.

The telephone rings and the man lunges, picks up the black receiver and listens: grunts, sputters, gurgles, a power line hums, limbs smack, flesh tears, flies bump glass and buzz, flesh rips, fabric torn, a multiplicity of tearing, of screaming, of men, of women, of creaking stairs collapsing, burning, of stabbing, of imploding glut.

The line dies, a thick buzz.

STATIC

Something bubbles from the bathroom.

The man boot-shuffles to the bathroom door, kicks it open, and slips on the wet tile. The shower is still running. Water coats the floor.

Behind him, though he has not yet seen her, Alina sits on the bed, cross-legged and pale-faced.

That telephone call as if torn to somewhere I've tangled before.

But a sudden pain clenches teeth. The man's chest cracks out static bone splinters. He's trembling. Can't help it.

"Love me, dear, don't think," Alina says. "Won't make it better, make it better."

The man blurts out a curse, spins, brow tense, mouth wide in horror.

It can't be her. It must be her.

"Weren't you just in the—"

"I'm always here," she says. "Come, Lek, sit."

The man hesitates, says, "I haven't seen you in so long."

"Don't lie," she says.

"The party at the desert house—"

"I'm not." She flexes her toes, leg dangling crossed over the other. She stretches them toward the television.

"What film is that?" And his voice wavers, fades.

"*You* should know," she says. She stands, too quick, and she's at the small table by the motel window, thumbing through a purse. She pulls out a pack of smokes, shakes one out.

"I don't know who I am."

"Are you ready?"

"I don't know," he says. But the words escaping his mouth sound wrong. He's ready. It sputters his imagination, this motel and this woman.

Alina inhales, exhales a stream of smoke. "Don't baby me, baby. This has been a long time coming. Here." She tosses him a keychain. It floats through the air and he opens his palm. It's there. "You better get going. This is your long time world, lover. Thought you disappeared."

"Me too," he says, not looking up at her. The key. "Where am I going?"

Alina laughs, walks back to the bed and sits down in the exact same spot. "Now's not the time to humor me with your baffled bullshit."

"But I—"

"Make me proud to be in love," she says.

Someone torched the bearskin. Patterns of puke like calligraphic smudges. A poetry of codes. More people fill the room to burst. The walls have turned semi-solid skin. Light flickers hard. Hot air whistles, moans like how Alina remembers Lek to smell, hotly stained with ink and hesitation. She flutters in the corner. She recalls windows. There are no windows now, no night air if it's even still night. A turn has come upon this stinky room. And Alina thinks she sees a wall split mouth-like and lick lips, split mouth-like and scream. Someone throws a blood-spattered camisole at the fireplace. Alina dives to retrieve it, bumps a hunk. She pushes aside a leather-masked gimp. Fingers curl around fabric, but it's not a camisole. It's a cardigan. She tugs it on, ignores the rumble. The floor is shifting stickier and she can't move right. There are no doors here. But to the left, screams as if space howls for the bodies to lie down, be swallowed. She keeps her eyes open, can't focus on the people in the room. No more false exits. And through fog and static, Alina smells argyle, piss, something earthy and familiar. Alina hugs herself, hugs the cardigan to her chest, wedges herself into the corner. Alina tries to hold her breath, but her lungs are tight. She chokes, hacks up burnt maggots, little black specks of ooze.

And someone chops into the room. The sound. The stench. The sight of a limb disconnecting from a body, from the body of a patsy, a construction. All she sees through the mess of bodies, through the smoke and the blood, is a shiny object hacking its way up and down and up and down and one voice towering screams over the others.

And Alina's vision is burst red.

The man's arm as machinated system, a process by which death is made possible, in which life is undone.

And even as she soundlessly utters the name of the man who

sinks in this gala, she no longer possesses a clear image of his face, such that she fails to realize that the man who is chopping the room to gory bits in this room full of blue static is Lek Gardenio.

A pink MG sports car shoots across desert asphalt.

Headlights hold curve upon curve of lonely road in twin circles of light.

Mash the gas harder.

Lek spins the dial. Old jazz fills the car.

Lek rounds yet another bend, heading higher up the mountain. Suddenly, he slams on the brakes. To his right, an automobile rages green flames and crackles about thirty feet off the road.

"Good Lord," Lek says.

He rushes to the flames.

"Anyone here?" he says. "Anyone alive?"

He bends, tries to see inside to the driver's seat. A cool desert breeze ghosts around his ears, buzzes. And through the shattered glass, Lek spies what appears to be a body in the tangle. The face has been glass-smashed, broken and splattered flat. He reaches in the cab to touch the body's fingers.

Lek stands, adjusts his suit coat, reaches into his slacks for something to smoke. He pauses. "If there's anyone out here, please answer."

He grips his temples, face scrunches, wrinkles in odd ways. He feels blood unloose in his nose, sucks it back up into his skull. And his vision is the vision of a woman in the wreckage. But he throws his arms into the air, exhales a swarm of flies that explode in tiny blood-drops in a moonlit The blood-drops form an arrow that point to a slope in the distance.

Lek is stumbling through the deep night toward the slope. Behind him, the car explodes, lights the sky orange.

And this is when he finds her.

But it's not her.

It's never her. He keeps following the blood. As if love were something one could stumble upon in the aftermath of a wreck.

But before Lek can make his way to the figure of a woman, a woman seemingly lying at the foot of a crooked tree, he is halted by a hand that slams down on his shoulder.

This is when the desert grows foggy, turns thick.

"Turn around, Lek," the voice says. "She's not real—not as real as you'll be, son."

"She's real," Lek says, still watching the woman. She appears to be sleeping, and he wants to run his fingers across her pale cheeks, to check for injuries, tears. "I've seen her before," he says.

"Look at me," the man says.

And Lek shuts his eyes, opens his mouth for the last of the flies to burp their way out. He sniffles the last of the blood up his head.

He opens his eyes.

Before him stands a priest.

"Father?" Lek says.

"Days getting shorter for you, eh?" the priest says. He pets Lek's black hair, studies his face like a man looking out at a mountain. "You've grown."

"I should—the blood—it's all in the . . . in the dirt."

"No dirt, son," the priest says. "Not where you're going."

"Who—?"

"A couple. No fuss for us, friend, not for my always friend."

"What did you say?"

"You got the jitters, the jitterbug shakes," the priest says. His arm drifts down to Lek's lower back, and he urges him to turn to face the fire of the exploded car. "We go this way. Places to be."

"And the wreck?" Lek kicks a rock.

"God's own pyromania."

"Has nothing to do with this."

"Has everything to do with this," the priest says. He stops Lek with his palm outstretched toward the flaming auto. "We all burn. In our own ways."

Lek's lips tickle with the blood flowing from his nose.

The priest pulls out a white handkerchief, "Blood of the lamb—blood to pass."

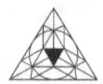

32

"And that's it?" Dallas says.

"That's that," Alina says. "Far as the eye can see—this one's a pawn."

Outside, the street light hangs through the window of the nearly empty cafe.

Two coffee cups and a white ashtray on the table. Fingers drum slow on the checkered Formica, Sinatra in the background. A barista towels off tables around them, whistles to the music. Outside, couples walk hand in swinging hand. Others pass with shopping bags, handbags, and backpacks, their bodies gracing the air through unheard conversations.

"All it took was a prod, huh," Dallas says. She pulls out another smoke, reaches across the table to Alina's side, near her cup, slides the lighter into her grip and lights it.

"Can I—?" Alina say.

"You quit, silly," Dallas says. "Not like it matters."

"In retrospect, I suppose," Alina says. "I quit every cycle. Probably ten minutes from now." They laugh. Alina lights a Viceroy, taps off the first ash, sucks smoke right down to her toes. "Really, it wasn't like that, not totally, but hard to put these things to words, right?"

"How old were you?"

"Seventeen, must have been—or, wait, older."

"Like a little deer."

"Like a little deer," Alina says. "But we all have these experiences, no? I can't be the only—" Alina's cell phone jingles from her purse.

"Work?" Dallas mouths.

Alina nods, answers "Hello" and says nothing. Her head bobs as if responding to someone important. She pushes out a "ung," to agree. Another to confirm. "Bye," she says. "Sure," she says. "It's okay," she says, hangs up.

"Who was that?"

"Nine to five unending."

"They work you."

"To the bone, babe—what are they thinking?"

"No more dream talk."

"Not tonight," Alina says. "Special case, he said—oblivious to pillow talk, obviously." She swallows the last of her coffee, hisses out a tiny burp. "They have more work, so I have more work, and no willows weep for me." She points to the ceiling, somehow signifying Sinatra's approval of her emotion through the synchronicity of that song.

"Not in this town," Dallas says. "You gotta go."

"I gotta go. Until tomorrow night. Eight?"

"Wouldn't miss it for any world."

"Our limo awaits," Alina says, stands, and holds out her hand for a smoke.

"For the road?"

"One vice."

"Tap, tap," Dallas says.

The office hall is empty this time of night. Lek grabs hold of the copier, pulls himself to his feet. He reaches for the first thing in sight, his coffee cup.

It stabilizes him, roots him to this reality.

The coffee is cold. It doesn't matter. He drinks it to the bottom, rubs at his nostrils. The bleeding has stopped. It's somehow darker now, something not right now. And Alina?

The Dark Room.

Floor forty-three. Stairs at the end of the hall, the elevator, or—that's it. Down below, he tries to recall what duties brought him up here in the first place other than to be able to snag a chat with Alina.

It's been a long time coming.

And the hallway. Something happened. It's been happening lately. To the point of concern. To the point of waking up standing, blade in hand, and shivering and shaking. First, it crept brainward in small doses like handling the butter knife out of the fork drawer, dipping the butter knife into the spread-tub, spreading the butter across toast, only to find the toast is not toast, but the throat of a blurred member sawn off. Or, take for instance, the simple gesture of crossing the room from the kitchen to the sofa. A subtle intent in the act. The feeling of letting one's body sink, become cushion. To imagine the result of the gaze from the sofa: the television, the window, the humidifier, the table. But, in this case, the crossing of the room, from the kitchen to the sofa crackles and hums, spits fragments and Lek finds himself in the middle of a night desert. The buzzing of flies.

"Calm yourself," he says to himself, but his voice pitches to the faintest shadow in the room. He focuses, but no one else is there.

It's in this dimming sensation in the copy room, here of all places, he first spots the photocopied flier for a celebration of grinding skin. So Lek jittered his hand over to the corkboard where the flier hung. And why hadn't he seen it before? He often visited the copy room, almost daily or nightly, and it had never been there. And he tore down the flier, held it in his hands. An invitation to tango. Come one. Come all. And the date, the date, the date was this evening, the evening of his awakening there in the copy room. "This can't be real," Lek says. "It is real, not real," Lek says.

He lifts his head. Somehow, in the spotting of the flier and the reading of the flier, he has drifted himself out into the hallway.

Lek folds the flier up, stuffs it in his pocket.

Lek shuffles down the hall, feels something brush up against his leg, something sharp in his pocket he must have forgotten about. Lek reaches into his slacks, pulls out a pair of scissors.

And the mutation of a motel room alters the soft spot of a dead man's mind.

The MG races further up the mountain. The priest sits beside Lek. They are winding higher and higher.

The priest passes him a pair of scissors, angles the twin blades between his legs. "Feel 'em crackle?" the priest says. "They burn when they hit your stomach. It's meant to purify, and you, son, need purification."

Lek hits a turn too fast, speeds up and guns toward another

dip in the road. "When I was a child," Lek says. "I thought why not, why not—"

"Live and let go," the priest says, holding his arm out into the night, beating back night air.

"But that's not true," Lek says. "I thought that was true. It was Delfonte and me, out back of Grandpa's barn. Where the secrets are."

"With whom, my good man?"

"Often Cindy, sometimes Josephine."

"Lovely."

"Lovely girl," Lek says. He swallows that mouthful of flies. "Until the day with the pitchfork—and Delafonte passed in a combine accident. Turned him into dog shit, it did. Can you believe that?"

"You wouldn't lie, Lek."

"Went out there drunk, he did. Drunk and left me alone with Cindy and Josephine. I was a real rattlesnake back in those days. Cindy ran off. Was how she called the sheriff, but Josephine, that hooter, she craved me real good."

"Angels exist," the priest says. "For troubled souls need to release steam. You did no harm."

"More than once," Lek says, hitting another turn too close to the edge, and the beams of his headlights hit only straight road now, just long and everlasting. Toward a house in the distance. "But Delafonte—too much of that snake juice, stupid gaping mouth and all, Josephine couldn't keep her trap shut about me letting him go, even he said he was just gonna horse around at old Stephanie Farante's place—fuck Stephanie Farante, I said— had too much myself." Lek laughs, grips the wheel harder, keeps talking: "Devil himself came down that day, spoke right in my ear, said let him go, so I let him go, was getting dark. Had your voice."

"Dark like tonight," the priest says. He pushes the scissors against Lek's genitals, rubs the handle against his bulge, feels Lek sprout.

Lek accelerates.

"We all do what we have a mind to do," the priest says.

"We do what we fucking do," Lek says, breath rushed. "And they never found her, boy did they go all flashlights and field walks; and ask stupid questions—was September or no, not yet leaves in the dirt—was why I left. As men do."

"Dirty men mess up," the priest says. He removes the scissors from Lek's crotch and places them on his own lap. "Don't you dare stop."

Ahead of them, not too far from the fast-moving automobile, stands a woman in the middle of the road. She waves her arms for them to stop.

Lek mashes the brake. The car fishtails out of control. He fights to keep it steady, to keep it from tumbling over the edge. The stench of smoke. The grinding brakes squeal a pig shriek.

His head slams against the steering wheel, the seatbelt cuts into his chest.

And the world is quiet.

The second floor.

Lek stumbles to the shag carpet stairs, wipes a stream of blood from his upper lip. He feels cold steel press against his lower back. The priest's mutter. The blood that has started as an intermittent tingle between the eyes has progressed to a nostril stream.

He cannot contain this fracture in his soul. He grips the wall, shakes his face and feels the rush of blood drizzle, drip all over the shag carpet.

It swells from his body in a glob.

There is no way out.

And the stairs are so close. Lek steps and steadies himself. He looks down to the bottom, sees the shadows of undulating bodies, the sound of flies swarming, singing, the stench of feasting. He steps unsteady, wavers. Lek cannot feel his toes, just nubs of throbbing pain and senseless guilt.

"Alina, I'm sorry," he says. "Forgive me for what I will do and do again until this night is through. I just—can't let you go, can't walk away from what we've got." Lek steps and steps, his arms steady him, a blind man teetering at the end of an erupted world. "We can go back," he says. "We can make this right."

But another voice cuts through the air of the house as if coming from inside him. It's the priest. Lek sees the man's image:

face broken and dented, cut open to reveal the swarming of flies inside of his empty skull, one eyeball rocking to the side.

"You forget the baggage you carry costs nothing but a life," the priest says. "Lucky you have me to usher you on, son."

Lek tightens his grip, but his hand tightens around cold metal—the black-handled scissors. "No," Lek says. "I don't want your shadow."

Lek turns his head. The priest stands behind him.

The priest laughs, reaches up and begins to peel off his face. Slowly. Screaming pitch-shifted screams; the squealing of pigs, a howling blaze—the crackle, the split wood. "Come, boy," the priest says, tugging at the skin, "there's still time to do what's right. You don't need her love—a body's a body of light."

Lek tries to drop the scissors, but he can't. It is as if they are glued to his hand. Sewn to the bone, melted to the skin. He forces himself down another stair, the priest following behind him. And below, from the first floor, the throbbing grunts of ecstasy swell and churn.

Lek looks back. The priest leans over the top stair, knifes out a trembling bloody hand toward Lek. "You need to do this—she doesn't care how I care," he says.

"I'm not listening to you anymore," Lek says, letting the blood flow from his nose and run down his lips, run into his mouth, so he can drink of himself and swallow the blood to the source. He can't stop the blood, can hardly see the next step down for the blood inside his head is at once rushing out of his body and filling his skull to rupture.

Too long has Lek stood in the shadow of the father.

For in that moment, the loss of feeling in his legs consume him and Lek statics, cracks his back on the shag stairs, much worse than a rug burn, for the pain is not a pleasurable scrape, and he still clenches the scissors, feels something swell up his spine. Lek's legs have grown mushy. He shuts his eyes, pushes his clumpy body down yet another stair with only a handful more to go.

"Don't look down," the priest says, "lest you slip off the edge again. I need you to do this."

But Lek cracks his mush-bones to stand and does look down

and he looks to the wall, tries to will his arm to reach that wall and steady him the rest of the way to the bottom, except the walls have gone and are filled with blood-soaked flies of light.

The hum of electricity, loud and endless. "What have you done to me?" Lek says.

"I have done nothing," the priest says. "I have only let you discover your own end."

"I never had a choice."

"So you'd think," the priest says. "Stupid boy! Filled to the brim with the unlived and the potential to do what you will, and look at you now—unbearable." The priest stomps on the shag. "Use the goddammned scissors, Lek. Slash some fucking throats."

This is when a crushing white wave of stench and steam blow down the hall, rush up the stairs, up to the second floor, a thick fog of human desire.

And the fog is the creation of a cowboy hat.

Lek's face throbs, tastes a rush of blood on his tongue.

"Do it for yourself," the priest says, sucking up those flies into his skinless face. "Set the world on fire."

Lek's hand twitches before him. He stares down at the scissors, somehow sharper now. He blinks away the blood and retches thick gobs on the floor. "Is this what you want?" Lek says. "This instrument in the hand of a maniac?" But when he turns again, the priest is all but a melting pile of flies and skin, blood and blackened bones of wind.

And the final spitting of the blood.

And Lek is a fountain of selves.

He gushes, steps, gushes.

Lek's eyes leak, bloodshot and burning. The abyss behind him, the abyss swelling all around him, shrieks him onward to the living room and the bacon cream dip.

Faster now.

He makes it.

His crooked gaze lingers, wobbly argyle feet stuttering in the hall.

He is a wolf among the dead and this is his homecoming walk to the finish line of glorious unbecoming.

One argyle foot after foot shamble through the hall of the living dead.

The return. Snip.

The ever lost. Snip.

He runs to the living room and lets it begin as it should.

Lek starts with a swing and a slash—not air—to flesh: sweat splitting, bursting to a bloody splatter. And the blood rivers out from Ray, his boss (or someone with the same pudgy disposition), until his neck is a hole. But the screams are worse than the priest's shriek: overpowering, shrill, a resonating drone.

Here is the chance.

And in the cutting and the chopping and the sawing and the screaming he feels the priest's vaporous blood-gush of skin and flies pushing him onward as wind pushes wheat, a gentle song of unbridled hate in his blood-stained ears, some sort of anti-hymn to help him drive those twin blades deeper into the skin of strangers, reach down to the floor and slice futilely at the veins that bind the house together.

Alina cringes in the corner: winter pale, shot-seed residue. Her beautiful face glimmers.

Something aches.

Her beauty is not a welcoming kind of beauty, but a horror. He was not prepared to be terrified. *It is not her*, he thinks. *This cannot be her*.

But he knows it is Alina. He knows he must continue the journey through the limbs and the cream, to pass her onto the way of the light.

And the priest is a simmering thud behind Lek's eyes. He's trying to pry his way in. Don't look. Keep pushing.

He pushes and drives the blade deep into the men and women he's fucked and been fucked by and this is the painful punishment. He must get to her. Not to save her. No. This has never been the quest. He pulls out the heart of a young woman and mushes it into her face so she can taste how love reeks.

"This is the letting go," Lek says to the woman as she falls to the ground. The doors to the room have been shut. A thick fog hovers from ankles and seeps up legs and coats skin in the presence of the priest.

STATIC

"No more doubt," the priest says. "It is time for you to become certain—plunge the blade." And Lek does. He tries to force his arms to stop the thrust of his blade, but the priest's words become the point of a different kind of blade, a familial blade of doing and undoing.

Lek lifts his head from a fresh kill and, yes, again, he feels Alina in the corner, still swarmed by the blurred outlines of men. He looks away. His body shudders once more and someone tears at his argyles. He raises the scissors, but she's pleading. Across the room, in the dark and the red and the blood and the pounding pain of the night, she's pleading for him to stop.

"Carry it out," the priest says, suddenly angry and impatient. He raises Lek's arm and forces it down again, forces it into the eye socket of a nearby man. "End her and set yourself free."

"I can't," he says.

"You must," the priest says. "Do it now."

And Lek raises the scissors again, slices. From deep within him, he smells the bleating of so many midnight sheep.

Lek throws aside a corpse and soaks in the beauty of the trembling and frightened Alina.

Static bleeds to a crackle. It's a bleating pig, a thundering sheep. The priest that is within Lek screams for him to slash. But Lek does not slash. The priest that is within Lek howls for him to butcher Alina. But Lek is not a broken saxophone, so he sputters out words and words that Alina does not understand.

"I can't—don't make me do this," he says. But she does not hear him. When he opens his mouth he is no longer human, he is a man made of flies. But it makes him. Lek's scream is so fierce, he rips the argyles right off his feet and his skin pricks, gouged, and hardens to a flat static of death-moans. "Didn't want you to see this," he says. "It's the only way."

"Don't do it, Lek," Alina says. "You don't have to do it."

But Lek cannot be sure she says what she says and if what she says is true, for his heart is not an organ that beats, it is a mangled organ in the church of a dead man. And the pain that throbs from the inside of his bloody skull cracks from the inside in an explosion of blood. And the explosion is a headlight under desert stars.

A woman's arms flail.

The car swerves off the desert road and the priest is thrown from the passenger seat. Lek reaches over, grabs the scissors. He guides the car to a sloppy stop, hops out and runs back to where the woman was standing.

She is still there, yet turned away from him.

The priest is nowhere to be seen. In the distance, off toward the light of a house, Lek hears laughter and moans as if they were close, but the distance is too much.

"Excuse me, miss," he says. "Are you okay? What are you doing out here?"

She tucks her hands into the pockets of her trench coat and turns to face him. It makes his knees jitter. He moves toward her. She says, "I was waiting for you, have always been waiting for you."

And Lek touches his nose. It is not bleeding. He moves to her. "You don't want to know," he says. "There are things—"

"I know, Lek," she says. "You don't have to explain."

"Don't think I can," he says. "But—"

"And where is your lucky lady?" She smiles something else behind her teeth. And Lek is suddenly dizzy. Maybe he hit his head too hard in the car. He clears his throat.

"Alina?"

"Yes," she says. "You knew I would be here."

"Where's the—"

"The gallows," she says. But that raging sound, that pulse is too much for Lek to handle. He grips the sides of his head and feels his brain melt to static nectar. The stabbing of a piano. The throb of a mallet on bare skin. He senses the sharpness of death from the handles of those black scissors.

"How can I make it stop?" he says, pleading with Alina, voice cracking in tears. "How can I silence this ache?"

"Open the trunk," Alina says.

And Lek stumbles over to the trunk, pops it open. A pair of argyle socks. He lifts them out and holds them up to the night sky. "How do I—socks?"

"You'll have to decide. Now, find me," Alina says.

And when Lek looks over to her, he finds himself alone.

Lek jumps back in the car, drives toward the house.

He floors the gas. Alina is in the passenger seat. Lek reaches over and strokes her shoulder.

"What if I don't like it?" she says, sheepish face, lip bitten, and earnest.

"Well, I don't really know how to answer that, I—"

"Have you been to one of these kinds of parties before?"

"First time for everything, I guess—"

"On a first date," she says, clasping her hands together. "Slow down."

"Think it started at seven. What time is it now?"

"I don't have a watch," Alina says. "Does it matter?"

"Just butterflies in my—" A fly hits Lek's chin. He swats it away, grits his teeth. Something in his head throbs.

"What's wrong?" Alina asks. "You don't look so good."

"No—I'm fine, maybe, hasn't hit me, yet. This taking you out. It's nice." He pauses. "Thank you."

They turn out of the surrounding emptiness into the driveway of a gigantic mansion. Lek pulls the car up next to another car and notices car upon car in the lot as if an entire small city were housed within.

Hand in hand.

To the end of a life.

And the front door creaks open. Lek and Alina both look up to that door, unsure who opened it, for the inside appears pitch black.

He strains his ears to hear sounds from inside the house, but he doesn't hear anything.

"What's wrong?" Alina says. "God, you're acting strange."

"Been here," Lek says.

He takes her hand and leads her up to the door. He sucks back more blood and quells the trembling inside him. Lek pushes the door open.

They look into the dark. The entry way is swollen with the sounds of moaning, of pleasure, drone out to the night. "I'm not sure if I want to," Lek says. "Captain Cold Feet, here." He tries to laugh it off.

"I'll be with you," Alina says. "Don't worry. You won't lose me." She winks at him and takes off into the black of the house, leaving him standing there at the entrance.

Alone.

It's darker without her and he is scared to enter.

This is when he feels someone over his shoulder, a force breathing thick. "Are you gonna enter or you gonna enter?" The man says. Lek jumps, startled beyond his expectations.

He hears a scream inside, male or female, he can't be sure, just a piercing wail.

"Alina?" Lek enters the house, the weight crushing him. His clothes are tatters. And there is nothing. This is not the copy room. He gropes for clean air, touches a pair of voluptuous breasts. The woman sinks her tongue down his mouth and they slurp. Lek lets the kiss consume him, then pulls away. He hovers near a fireplace: limbs and tongues, cocks and crows. The entire place stinks. The ceiling puckers, winks.

A voices call out and that voice is smothered cum, a gurgle from another world. A chant fills his ears. Lek looks down at his body. He is coated in prickly static. It is not the kind of static one can pass a hand through, the kind that blurs the world to a kind of snowy background. This is a static of thundering noise and bone.

"Help me," he says. No one hears him. A woman wraps arms around him as he dissolves into her skin and is sucked up inside her. He messily tumbles out her mouth only to find that he's enjoying the feeling of sucking her nipples. She squeezes his throat. He hears a drill from another room, the sound of a whip cracking skin. Oiled men surround him, sword tugging and yelling. They jeer at his naked body.

Lek tears himself away from the woman, rushes down a dim hall. The lights are red and dark and flickering on and off and he suddenly doesn't know how to find the exit. A man stands deeper down the hall—faceless and blurry—with the smock of a priest and touches himself lewdly. Lek tries to stand but a woman forces him onto a bed, ties his wrists and ankles together and mounts him. Rope burns through his argyle socks. No pleasure, there is nothing pleasurable about the restraints and the hell he has found himself in.

STATIC

"Lek . . . Lek . . . ," he hears a voice cry out from behind a wall, but the voice is drowned in piss. He tries to sit up. A rubber-masked woman rubs herself in his face and he's drowning in her body, again, lost in the dunes of a body. To burst. Filled with empty light. He feels the tip of his head crackle and wants to vomit blood, but the blood hardens in his throat. Cement. Lek struggles at the ropes and buckles and thrashes. Another woman straddles him and she squeezes her lower muscle-pit to suck him up inside her.

A way out.

This, he thinks, *is also a way out.*

Lek screams, chokes out more life. It's one of the onlookers. They are spitting all over his face, pushing wet gush into his mouth and over his nose. Blood gushes from his holes and he hurts and he cries. Too much for one man to bear. A wishing well of flies, a throbbing of voices overlapping and oozing into each other.

"Get me out of here!" he yells. His wrist comes untied. Lek throws a fist, hits air. The women undulate wildly. One of them cracks a whip, smacks it across his legs. Argyle burns his feet. He scrambles to the corner, holds his hands in front of him, jittering his fingers as if some faux magic trick would rescue him from the agony. The whip cracks again, stings his pepper-tree and burns up into his skull. He sneezes blood, coughs tiny flies all about the room. He thrashes around and rams into the bodies that surround him. "Where's Alina?" he cries. The eyes of the onlookers cringe. He hears a man scream. Fingernails crack, rip. The ceiling sags.

Lek lunges forward, out of the room and into the hallway.

The light in the hallway is cold, bright. He hears slop, smells bacon from the living room. And no one follows him into the hall. He leans back, catches his breath. Others drizzle through the walls. An orgy of moans, yelps, curdles. Lek drags forward, across the hall to the other wall. He comes to himself, lets his heart beat seep out from the tip with a deathly shiver.

To the heart of a slaughter.

Lek's scissors splatter skin, sink to chop lungs and extract. He shoves another man aside, tries to look away from Alina. She sobs mercy before him, an angel before him. He slams the scissors against his leg, just beats them there.

"You can get us out of here," Alina says. "You can do it, Lek. Please."

But the house is a muscle around them. It is not a beautiful mansion. It is not filled with the men and women of his life. The harder he tries to look at the people around him the more he smells shit and piss and carrion in an abattoir. And the house is not a deserted shack one can burn, forget and flee forever. Lek raises them over his head.

"I'm sorry, Alina, that it's come to this, things are not as they seem and I want out."

"Don't, please—God, no please," she pleads, holds her beautiful hands up over her beautiful face and Lek spies her eyes through the webs of her fingers and clenches the bloody blades.

One swipe and he could do it.

One swipe and she'd be over and this would be over and he would finally be the man he knows the priest wills him to be.

Lek remains covered in blood. And his nose leaks a steady stream of blood. And he looks down at his cock. It is hard, beyond hard, has never felt it so hard before. It is space itself. It is dirt and rock and mud and animal. And Alina cries a cry like a dying dove. Lek looks down at this precious dove as if he would never harm a bird, but a static version of himself as a skinless bag of flies pushes him to slam the blade into her skull. The blade shines in the dim red light of the living room. Lek smells the bodies of the dead.

"I can," he says.

"You can," Alina says. "Mercy, Lek."

Lek blinks, a form of shutting out. Lek blinks, the past is not really the past and in his blinking he savors the motel room, that monster of his own creation.

"Don't kill me," Alina says. "This isn't you."

"It's a way out," he says.

STATIC

"We can make this work," Alina says, but her voice does not come from the voice of the screaming Alina. It is a voice of ugly static as if somehow she has filtered herself through a television set's tinny speaker. This infuriates Lek. He just wants to hear her say something real, something clear and he focuses on her strawberry-sweet hair, on that point of her head that must be the tip of her skull.

"Nail her, son," the priest says, the warbling imitation of a man. Alina shrieks.

Lek turns old blood. "I will not listen to you," Lek says. And in that moment, he births the death of himself. The skin-shell and genitals of the others melt into air and a new form of static pulses up from his feet, and it's hot, but not a hot that burns or stings. It is real and timeless. He cracks his neck, ungrits his teeth and trills out a flute-line from his new mouth. "I will never—"

Lek quickly lowers the blade and brings the blade to his meat-rock, to his stiff dick, to the throb. He opens the twin blades of the scissors and places the point where they meet around his penis and now both hands hold the handle.

"Don't disobey yourself," the priest says. "I can give this to you, you son of a bitch."

Alina's face ruptures a sly smile.

And the birth begins.

Lek grunts, forces the scissor handles shut and the blades grind into his dick, severing skin, but not fully slicing through. Black blood gurgles thick from the wound. He is filled with terror, consumed by the abyss. It is a clarity of static that drains him pale. Lek hears the trumpet call, the death drums. He squeezes again with more strength and saws at the rigid vein-laced skin soup dangling now limp from his groin.

"You ruined everything," the priest says, but his voice is sinking and wavering to nothing at all.

Lek roars, wrenches at the handle again, sawing and chop, chop, chopping into his own member with hate and crunching blood, snip by snip. Those among the living that surround him are screaming and pleading, moaning and melting. He saws, grinds the blade through the bloody meat and lops off his penis, watches it flop flaccid on the floor.

And this is when man becomes river.
This is when man becomes lover.

The house is a bloodbath.

No one moves, except Lek, who towers over Alina. He's bleeding out from the crotch. Alina scuttles back ever farther. Too much gore and this was not her idea of redemption.

"Oh, Lek," she says. "What did you do?"

"This is not about me," he says, digging the scissors further up his mangled midsection and wrenching out a clump of his own insides. More bloody parts of him fall to the floor and he hunches over, tries to look inside himself.

But something bubbles up from Lek's snipped and mangled middle.

Alina takes pause, covers her mouth, can't shut her eyes, can't bear the stench of what lies under Lek's opening skin.

It begins with his fingers digging into the fleshy hole of his wound. Lek howls, slams the scissors, blades-deep, into that mushy hole and he digs up, tears skin up his stomach like a mad doctor in surgery with himself.

Alina doesn't know how to comprehend this, or the look on his face, how he shuts his eyes, or the light bubbling within him with each wrenching tear of the scissors.

Slice up.

And the sound of static shatters the room. It's coming from the veined walls, the sound of blood pulsating. The floor has turned fleshy and the upper levels of the house have vanished, are replaced with the night sky, stars circling and popping to dust.

"This is all," Lek screams, and inside him there are no more words. Each rip of the blade (through guts, through lungs) is a flash of the priest dissolving in a pile of mush on the floor. Lek squints, grits teeth and feels the force of his priest-father dull and flatten. The old bastard, the old bastard's words and words and words, too many to bear, too much to swallow.

Lek swallows, spits more blood, but keeps sliding the blade inward, slicing himself open. He is making a passage for Alina to escape.

STATIC

And Alina is stricken on the floor, sweat-covered, and shivering. She cannot look away.

Lek's chest splits open.

He throws down the scissors. They land on a pile of mush, a bloody collar destroyed.

Lek stumbles forward a step. His entire chest is an open wound. But, all is not what it seems.

The inside of Lek's body is a sea of static.

The house rumbles, shakes and a crack splits the floor from behind them. Bodies slip into the vortex.

And he digs his hands inside himself, further splits his chest wide open. A swarm of flies shoot from inside him. This is when Alina sees the road.

A monochromatic road stretching out to dark. It's a television screen inside him.

She crawls forward, pushes herself to her feet and sways. "And what if I don't?" she says. "What if this is all a lie, Lek? I looked for you . . ."

"It's not a lie," he says, forcing back the blackening of his vision as he strains to hold himself open. "Come inside . . . Please, Alina. Come inside."

"I can't," she says, but her words are buried in a snap of wood and concrete. A gigantic crack severs the ground around her. She falls back against the wall, feels its pull. Fleshy tentacles ensnaring her in goop. She tears herself free. Lek screams, digs his hands even deeper within his body, legs buckling, blood pouring, and gapes himself wide.

And those fleshy walls clot and slime over with static-skin.

Alina screams, splatters head first into Lek's torn-open hole.

He widens his stance, angles the gap open for her to enter and feels her become him. She pushes her body inside, past the static and the muck and the flesh and the blood.

"Thank you," Lek says. "Thank you for love."

Ding Dong. Lek opens the door. He's wearing a green cardigan and khakis, a corncob pipe clenched between his lips. Soft jazz wafts from his living room and behind him several guests mingle around the kitchen and the dining room.

"Here she is," he says. "Right on time."

"Sorry, I'm late," Alina says. "Rush hour."

"Nonsense, come in. You look wonderful. Let me take your coat."

Someone taps Alina on the shoulder. It's Dallas.

"Dallas?" Alina says. "Hey-o, how's it going?"

"Just got here. Congratulations."

"Thanks, dear. God, you're probably the only one who really gets this whole affair."

"The messier the better," Dallas says. "You know that. I'm here for you, here for both of you."

And Lek wraps an arm around Alina. "You never told me you had such interesting friends," he says. "Dallas, drink?"

"What do you got?"

"Whatever you need."

Ding Dong. More people are arriving and Lek turns, motions for Dallas to get the door. Behind him, the kitchen is a-buzz with office folks and a host of others Alina has never seen before in her life.

"Dinner's ready," a girl yells out. "Serve yourself."

"Gotta mingle," Lek says. "I'll catch up with both of you later."

Soon, the front door opens. A family of three enter. The music shifts to some kind of Latin groove, bongos, and trumpet trills. The twist. The pony. A guy puts a drink in Alina's hand. She hears someone scream, catches a glimpse of Lek in the kitchen with a meat cleaver. He's carving up mutton. Always was a sucker for mutton. *Ding Dong.* More people pile in. Alina is pushed back to the dining room. Plates clink and clack. She steps on a spoon. Dallas is nowhere to be seen.

"Lek?" she calls, but so many people are now crowding the front room, she can't manage to get to the kitchen. "Lek, I need to talk to you."

Someone turns on the television. A wave of static overtakes the Latin groove for a second, but pitters to nothing. More people stumble in. "There a party in here?" "Heard something about meat?"

STATIC

And a feast has been laid out before Lek. It's a divine spread. He rubs his eyes. Alina sits next to him, pours him a glass of red wine. "This'll help, dear," she says.

"Thank you." But Lek's head throbs, pulses, crackles.

Dallas whispers something into Alina's ear. Alina smiles, raises her glass. "Thank you for coming, everyone." The other dinner guests raise their glasses for a toast. Lek is shaking, but he raises his glass.

From where he sits in the dining room, he can see the living room and it appears someone's left the television on, but it's just static.

"To my wonderful Lek," Alina says. "I know it's quick, but neither of us believe in using time as our measuring stick, especially when it comes to matters such as these." She takes a deep breath, huge smile. "To the best man I know. My future husband. I love you."

And with raised glasses, the dinner guests clink and drink. Lek snaps back to reality, tongues a sip, but the pain is too much. "I'll be right back," he says. He stands, kisses Alina on the forehead. He bends down to her ear. "Thank you, dear. It's wonderful. You're wonderful."

Lek walks to the living room. The place is a mess of food scraps, cups, and discarded clothes. He smells shrimp dip and bacon cream. Alina laughs, a cackle through the walls. He smells ash. More glasses clink to laughter.

Lek kneels down by the television and stares at the static as if forced.

He slowly reaches his hand out, trembles fingers down the plasma screen. He catches sight of himself—a monster, a ghost—in the static. Made of static. A split second jolt. In the static, he is blood-covered, chest ripped open, swarming flies.

Alina cackles louder from the dining room. The sound of forks and knives scraping plates, shoveling meat to mouths.

Lek could reach inside that screen and disappear. He touches his face, wanting it to be real.

The static on the television set is a night desert. He wants to sink into it, anonymous, grey. He shuts his eyes and feels selves of himself bubble, fester. He feels his cock stiffen and he breathes harder, faster, harder, harder.

A way to disappear.

Just walk back into the dining room and eat your food.

"No more," he says, and Lek punches the television as hard as he can, spiderwebbing the plastic plasma into jagged chunks. He punches it again, knocks the television back against the wall. Broken.

Chairs scoot. Grunts. Grumbles. Silverware clatters. Lek trembles. People rush to him.

Suddenly, the dinner guests fill the room. Lek topples, flat on his back, clutching his fist. "I'm sorry," he says to Alina. "I destroyed . . . it's—I'm gone."

Alina, kneeling beside him, scoots in, places his head on her lap. She whispers: "You don't have to destroy anything."

Blood pounding in Lek's chest.

A stirring.

"Maybe I am just a desert," Lek says.

"My desert," Alina says. "Tell me what happened."

"I'll tell you," Lek says, tearing up. "I'll tell you everything."

The other guests move back and give them space.

The television sits smoking with a fist-sized hole in it.

"Whatever's haunting you, Lek, it's over."

"I know . . . " he says, sobbing. "Thank you."

"Close your eyes, close your eyes and sleep."

"Everything's going to be okay?" he says, voice slurring and slipping.

Dallas passes Alina a wadded up dish towel. "Your scalpel, doctor," she says.

Alina nods, carefully unwraps the towel, careful not to damage what lies wrapped within.

She unveils a pair of black-handled scissors, raises them for all to see.

"Take off his pants," Alina says. "Let's do this while he's down."

ORGONE

A STAGE, the remnants of a black box theatre—gutted cellar, dirt-brick ceiling and floor grime, the building just a drooping obelisk among toppled roofs, scattered rubble. Hear boots and bare feet slump down crumbled slats, shuffle unto a clearing of cinder block chunks and crates for seats.

Golo is already there, pacing, fingering shapes in the dark theatre's dirt.

A bubbling vat near the center, fire-lit, smokes yellow sizzles.

More observers trickle in, shiver and chatter and twitch. Golo slouches to a side room, a tunnel leading back up to the snow; his final preparation for the evening's spark.

If done right, with precise ferocity, the night's performance strives to erase grime from the gathered crowd by way of Golo's controlled contortions, chants, and whip cracks. The art of ritual cleansing.

He studies the outside terrain. His thoughts of grandeur sink to scattered bruises under the surface—the flittering ache of a showman, a shaman, a sharpened hermit about to step, to dissolve himself in art. To heal.

Outside, the sky is barren, the carrion birds long dead.

His stubbled head bows and he squats, pulls open his coat, dips fingers far into a pooling glob of coral-hued tissue that gurgles jellied pockets of heat, a pool he's been monitoring for days and the properties the pool takes and gives: a dollop of nectar from a city girl's finger, a scrap of pinafore, burial dirt, blood red.

A branch beside him. A woodblock. A whipping switch.

The smell of rot rising in the air.

The smell of octopus brain matter.

He scoops the octopus brain into his palms, butters mollusk divinity onto his face, stringing it through his beard, over shut eyelids, down brow and all about the back of his skinny neck, his bony chest and lumped muscles, veins, wrist-bones, to the tip of his head, until his upper body is smothered slick with warm brain.

The pink simmers, burns white, molds hard to his skin.

Golo's spine shudders.

He strips himself of the thick-threaded *hakama* dress, black suspenders and boots. Shivering bare, he smothers his whole body in the ancient mass of the leviathan, for the leviathan's brain stretches for miles upon miles. The entire plain, even the burning city itself, rests upon the lopped-open skull of this ancient frozen beast.

The air drips colder—Golo's love buried in mountain remnants, trinkets and fire—landscape as inner repetition of loss.

From the cellar stage below, acrid fumes waver from censers. The act's foundation, Misao's piss mixture, bubbles in the vat, the stinky crackle of her bottled expulsion to massage, penetrate the crowd's now fevered chatters, and to cleanse the crowd. Let the process begin.

The mollusk brain has taken effect.

Golo retrieves his garments, winces—a rupturing stab splinters his vision, stabs at his spine—body thrust to focus on a quad of hulking shapes in the outer distance. Four men, he thinks. He stiffens, suddenly seared from the inside out.

He knows those men see his convulsion.

Golo is mesmerized by the impenetrable psychic force of their distant trudge. They are lumbering toward where the north hill crests to the suctioned slopes beyond—a place of no inhabitance for the four or for anyone who knows better.

And there must be incense, thick bundles. Four trails of tangled smoke-lines. The echo of a low-toned temple bell's ring still pinging off their gongs as if creating a soundtrack to the discomfort Golo feels now that he knows they are there.

And perhaps this sudden discomfort is the seepage of the brain transforming Golo's body, how for those trained in the art of psychophysical therapeutics, the brain-smeared body gains entry to the door to become the unconscious's diamond-breath sensing: carrion projection, the poetry of death, a medicinal lucidity. But a wet force stings Golo's gut: a crack like a thick blade or a bludgeoning hilt, torn muscle exploding. He struggles not to scream; he grunts, folds over, can't speak. Pain blots his sight to dots—a glob of fissures stabbing against his chest.

His veins bubble.

Of her, his Ami, so clear is her image, dear Ami.

And Golo wrenches at his body, struggles to straighten, must grip, press palms to his heart lest he tears off the layer of brain-skin, drain dead in the snow, be haunted by his wife's death once again.

A hum shivers the ears. Must come from the jaw, from the snapping gong. It strikes yet. Harder. Face muscles tighten, hold. He grips his own face by the gums and yanks. *Crack*—jaw snaps sideways, opens and he can breathe, lets the pain ball on his tongue.

Resist.

And steady, grounded.

The temple bell pings once more.

The piss stench spreads out from the hole behind him, a beckoning. Inhale Misao, he thinks. And summon, don't waver toward potential danger.

But Golo, as if in the natural order of actions to be acted upon, shuts his mouth and strains to breathe the smoke of the four men's near distant linger if only to gain what secrets they carry. He blanks, sucks air like an addict, a whistle.

And holds them close.

Can't place their origin nor purpose, these four.

No signal to speak.

A blocked connection.

And the sense of being exposed from afar—vultures plucking out the eyes of a blind man, guts ripped open. A flash of red revolving, crashes. He squints out the pain.

Who are you? he thinks, and watches them float forward.

And is seen.

Beyond, those four sets of eyes glow through the purpled dark, slinking through the snow, journeying, disappearing with their heads turned toward Golo.

The jaw again. Open it. A constricted omen.

From over the crest, their temple bell pings harder, a sting on the top of his head. Golo shudders confusion, nails pricking skin, and quick, turns, retreats toward the opening in the building lest he loses the mollusk magic brewing over his body.

Lest he admits his weakness in the face of the unknown.

And the shapes and sounds of the four have passed beyond the hill.

All is still. He faces that crest, perhaps to hear more and takes a step. He reaches out, withdraws, bends and hurries to gather his clothes in a heap.

Misao's soft hand touches his shoulder. He jerks. And how long has she been standing there? She's always so quiet when not entranced, God's own blip. "Your time," she says, thinking him merely wandering the chamber of his mind or some such inner solitude. "The beyond awaits."

But that smell and that sound, Misao, thinks Golo, his face to the sky, may possibly be the commencement of our glorious future of pain.

A wooden chair is placed in the center of the cellar space.

Construction of the dead.

The black box stage with its rubble slats, dirt and concrete stains, surrounded by a barrage of head-bent seekers in ragged coats and boots, resounds with the echoes of their grunts and mumbled-jumbo. A white light illumines the chair.

A candle burns white.

Misao slides a microphone stand into place as a prop. She twists the stand tight, clicks on the mic, and steps to the side. Her piss bubbles and spits, tremors the room with her stink.

Golo enters soundlessly with a penetrating smell from a hole in the wall, still blocking the shrinking pain inside him, and, placing himself in front of the chair, owns the stage, as he should. His smothered body glows, sickening, whiter.

He raises his head, inhales, but does not summon and explode the crowd's fervor. Instead, with a secret mantra only he perceives, he opens the electric brainwaves of his medicinal art, coated in the doctored slime of octopus meat seeping, and sits.

Preparation for the art.

He sits on the wooden chair, Golo, a naked man of an undeterminable age, scalped, pale, and bearded, doused poetic, with fingers firmly placed on his lap—a vibration to summon lotus light, a lust conjurer, fog eyes a swirl of purple, and thus it begins. And he speaks wires of non-words, a warped mantra, an inhalation, exhalation embodied, churning labored and mumbled and on and in and on. Expunged breath as oscillation. In. An engine mingled with the hum of an active power line. The branch, a whipping switch unbroken, gnarled and in. Whole.

Suck on and in, a mutilated orchestra of moans.

Breathe, Golo, breathe and spread deeper, breathe out and heal to—the sanctum, the pineal, the temple bell, and burn the sea, become form—the periphery unveiled.

A crack.

He stands, already twitching, rooted, contorted, voice strangled like a field of bellowing beasts.

Misao drops her top: twin moons and buttons, arms raised as if to penetrate his current.

Golo's screams suddenly twist the room.

The onlookers and their heels, their crusty boots and callused feet have taken to epileptic shuffles, stomps, crackled shocks—moans of the sick, bellows of the heavy hearted.

A crack.

Space sinks.

The whipping switch to Misao's chest, navel, thigh, knees, and heart. Her voice birding dirtward. It trills, flocks flutter, and she prepares for the gush, a rush of poetry.

Prepares for power itself to twist and manifest.

Golo feels the pit of the mollusk conjoin to the messenger. And the crowd, at his command, reels with the snapping of bone-breath, the unshedding of ontological armor. All lips and teeth splintering, melting, flowering.

He wants to obliterate. He wants the mercy of his dance to choke their breath so they may breathe afresh the air of this wretched mountain. A blizzard to sew. Of ether and orgone dreams. Slaughtered love as catharsis.

Push and breathe. The seed births his hands to flutter, splatters waves of air from his pores.

A crack.

The crowd bloats, floating side to side.

Misao is bent. Her entranced screams. Her screams dip, entwine the crowd.

And sudden.

The stench of her mystical piss.

But Golo senses a split—an unnatural welt chewing his body, blocking the flow of energy.

Something grinds inward from the back of his skull.

Turn, pucker the second act. He whips Misao's feet and up to her ass, drives welts around her spine. Her voice bolts the crowd from the inside out, feeds Golo's prayer with her feasting screams. The wooden chair rattles. A pulsation of pink matter expanding, sucking dirt from lungs.

The room burns piss, strings of vinegar, the smell of soiled cloth.

Tongues cluck and clack and the crowd clenches fists and stomachs, throats of broken glass. You, the breath. Humanize light—no, the split widens, flattens his tongue, expands. An axe blow from elsewhere—push it away.

This is Golo's conjuring.

The blow smashes through skin. To bone.

And the pain crashes through Golo's neck, not what he was expecting.

Is there someone projecting, psychically tapping in the room? Golo strains to see, can't see.

This shouldn't be happening. A wrenching screw twisting, sears his throat.

Golo spasms, jerks, his mantra, a sputtering growl.

A crack.

Misao spreads herself and squirts screaming louder, topples the chair.

A man near the front vomits toward the stage as if the crowd, too, can feel his pain.

Golo can breathe, but in spurts, in little bubbles.

The fine sour evaporating under the pain of whatever disruption is occurring.

And Misao hums to Golo, her ritual song, a stopping point. Golo raises the whipping switch. A red beam blurts out his face. The rotten hovering of skin decaying, dropping from faces in clumps.

He drops the switch. Fingers needle, cramp.

Misao kneeling, grabs the switch and cracks it repeatedly on the ground—a snap, snap, snap, snap, snap, snap—and furthers the action to a calming of breath, heaving chest slower, slower drips of air.

But the crowd moans and heaves against her and spits the vomit of their unease all over the floor. A human sea of imagined pain. A transference.

This excruciation is not part of the ritual. Something has gone wrong. Golo struggles to regain control of his mind, block the agony from spreading deeper. A woody smoke melts his mouth. And the hum of electricity melts into the bubbling coo of Misao's piss—the piss, become the piss. She shrieks louder, yipping—an incantatory scream as if she knows Golo's exaggerated flails, eyes wide open, are not part of the act. Golo collapses on the ground and this is the struggle:

A pineal prick widening bluer.

An opening of the cranial vertex.

Golo raises his arms, drops, and worms in a circle on the floor on his back.

The droop of his face, the sheer blankness and his mouth wider, jaw popping from bone to scream louder—to become one with the hum of the electricity and the piss.

And the tortured bliss of it all—he sees her. There, he sees her, his love.

A crack.

Brain seeped inside, rushes to blot the intrusion.

A speck of memory. His mirror self at the shack in the icy woods of their love. It's Ami. Her fingers of love and guidance rest on his shoulders, slide up and down and knead, unknot muscle ropes, tighter. She bends to his ear, is speaking to him of a holy heat in the dark. She releases her grip. Golo's fingers reach across the table. There is a book lying open—rich paper, ink smudging, splotching.

And suddenly, his memory of the bursting open of the wooden door.

The scream, sudden stench, the wetness of death.

A force slams into skin.

Ami's hot blood pours from the top of his head, goops life

down his face. Her body crushing hot and stolen by a blow, crushing his lungs against the desk. He turns to the glint of an axe head in the moonlit dark—a streak, stained with her gore. He is smattered in Ami's blood, in her shriek. Slop up. Beyond. And Golo struggles to stand, but his wife's body is a brick-hued skin broken. His face is mashed into the book on the table from the force of her collapse, tongue caught between his teeth, too quick to act. And the chops sound thrice. And the crack.

If he could open his mouth, he would scream.

But to whom? For the blunt end of the remembered axe strikes him to the ground, thuds him to sleep.

A crack.

Misao's gash flowers a sweet mist, coats the room.

The crowd is all but a heap of spasming bodies, sweating out the sick and shivering, full of cramps exploding.

The piss has bubbled to a black goop boiling in the vat.

Misao cracks the whipping switch harder, trying to force Golo out of his ethereal misery.

She holds his blank eyes with her prayer as if unchaining him from whatever shackle possesses him.

Golo stands, steps backward left foot directly behind right foot. He's pressing against himself. To cease the fright. Right foot steps directly aligned with left foot. Eyes crusted, blurry. Can't make out any interference from the crowd. A shuffling darkness. Focus on the feet. And repeat. To love again. And appear. To the chair. To the chair and sit.

It's fading.

All dropping.

He slowly, deliberately sits, lips mutter the ending, stress the final syllable—a long o, and lets that vowel stutter.

Become heat.

Quiet.

Stilling.

Misao hands him the whipping switch, not sure of where his mind went or to what extent he still has it at all, but the crowd withers and claps. Some collapse in shouts of thanks, others obviously confused.

Golo places the switch in his lap, picks the branch up off the floor.

The branch has turned burnt black.

He swallows—yes, the pain was real—brain dissolving, chipping off his skin in flakes like sheets of ice.

And cracks the branch in half.

A temple bell pings off Golo's tongue. He breathes it out, tastes orgone.

Tastes the New.

Meditation—phase one—complete.

Memory and pain spawn elevated states. A necessary intrusion, Golo fuck-meditates Misao rough—louder—her spinal nubs curved, body bent over the wooden chair in the black box—to reflect. To detach. Three stragglers from the crowd—their rags waft mold—drool from a sticky dirt corner, grunt and fondle.

The rhythm—like the click of a woodblock—nurtures, nurses the pain of the performance.

If the shapes moving to the horizon meant anything to Golo, they embodied an answer. Like the night of his wife's slaughter. He's come to swallow her death in lumps. It was the summoning pen-stroke for them to resign their efforts to utilize the orgone energy believed to be trapped in the octopus brain-dirt of the mountain—orgone, itself: life-element of the lotus and the diamond, yolk and the seed.

A letter followed days later, knived to his door on a frigid night. The script was not of a tongue Golo could read, well read as he is. No footprints marked the way. Enflamed by grief, he burnt the letter in a vat of boar's blood and bat shit, breathed a divination to Kala, and chose to bury his wife (he had kept her body under a tarp behind the shack for study) on a hill near their home. Schematics stolen, her work gone the way of ash—by way of the axe slaughterer, no doubt—and void of clues, leads, confirmations, or crumbs to suck after, Golo remained alone, brooding until the night of Misao's occurrence.

She claimed to have fled from a desert commune, a simple ceremonial girl of bruised elbows, half-sewn scars and sorrow, likely to end up gutted or bled out by the blade of whatever surgeon would buy and dissect her. A maiden unleashed. Misao ran to the edge. She had squeezed her skin through layers upon twined layer of barb-wire, glass bits, and the gut-chunked shards that sang of a way out.

Now, as Golo juices her divine form, he suffers a rush of grandeur, a paroxysm, an awakening storm—together, they would rekindle the orgonotic operation in secrecy, resume construction of the accumulator from memory, and melds its mystery to his artistic rituals for the purpose of preserving his dead wife's life work—his dream-splattered bride would live on.

He pinches himself shut and pulls out, thumb sharp on the hilt and shoots sleet across her back, blotting his thoughts with a trace of orgone. He would study the grace of expulsion, a way to transcendence, scrape revolt from the floors and the brain, more and more, and begin with the effects of whatever fraudulent sorcery those night wanderers had pushed into the depths of his alchemical art.

For Ami.

Bending, Misao strokes, slops him against her teeth.

Golo breathes. "We need a sack for the puke," he says. "Accumulate—tomorrow, we build."

She looks away, spits a glob of Golo to the floor. But Golo, already peeling at the brain, does not return home on this terrible night.

Coated and booted, the dark paints Golo thickly cold.

Misao's soft patters, vomit-sack dragging behind her, have since been swallowed by snow and night.

Alone, Golo trudges to the crest, woodblock and whipping switch in hand, to follow the prints of the four who came before.

He lets the snow turn pink in his mind, a mind-tunnel to conjure the memory of the shack. Of the infiltration. And it's the ping of that bell, once again, filling him to trudge. To seek. But no more. No more than a vague brush; Golo's mind vibrates.

Boots stick in the snow. He rips up on his leg, wipes off the stuck coral matter and staggers to a standstill just as the crest peaks to a most unnatural sight.

A giant naked woman the length of a slender ship, lies toes-extended-upward in the snow as if asleep. Or fallen. Unburied, palms up and perfect nails. Her pale skin shimmers a dull grey, long locks of hair streak outward from her head, snow-whipped, tips frozen and shimmery. All around Golo, a buzz, a snap swarming. Pink brain tissue leaks up around where her body lies. It smells of sage. He cups his ears and smacks his whipping stick in the snow, trying to study the pattern of disruption as prediction.

Nothing, just specks he can't see and chattering teeth.

The dead energy of the giant woman beckons him near. A woody smell. Of caverns.

And behind, from the ruined city, a booming of brick, muted dull and deep, but that is miles away—hot fire and piles of rot.

It's on the wind, this night.

Yet, as a professor in the academy, years before, Golo spent an orange autumn studying various forms of the unidentified phantasmagoria of the world, a plateau in his life where he believed himself a witness to haunts, zips, and skittering pirouettes. Sky legions of invisibility. Krakens like monoliths. Perhaps, he thinks, this whale of a woman is a creature—a specimen of sorts, made of art. But who would place such a creature on the outer edge? In the brained snow. An undecorated glimpse.

Of perfection.

Golo moves closer to the giant girl. She lies on her back, arms outstretched, fingers spread spotless, save for two bloody gashes on the side of the girl's chest, just under her right breast. A hum expanding. The crushed snow. Boot prints. Someone or something has scaled the giant's chest.

Dig fingers into skin and climb. And he does. Golo scales the woman's side, up around the breast—an iced nipple beacon—and to the heart, but the heart is a sawn open hole leading down.

Golo listens. Snow sprinkles, falls scattered, melts on the inside of the body.

And there beside the hole, a spread of ashes lies faintly smoking. Golo crouches, inhales the perfume to confirm the four strangers who must have already descended.

It's a heady blank swirl at this proximity.

A hallucination of Ami stands before Golo, her face gashed open from the tip of her head, split through her left eye—a creamed yolk—to the middle of where her nose once was. She's wearing the dress of her death-date. And behind Ami is the orgone accumulator of his shamanistic vision cast with the faint shadow of Misao's face from inside the small glass window on the accumulator's door.

Ami's head tips back and back, face up to the sky.

And a speckle of snow, just one dancing crystal, hits the smoking ember that Golo inhales like a pig, and snuffs it out.

Snuffs Ami—her trance body ripped, decimated to white fluff and blood vapors. To snow.

But the sound has shifted. Somewhere inside the giant girl's body, Golo hears the ping of that gong, a throat-song fevered with yip tones and growls—the clicking of a stick. He picks himself up, tugs his *hakama* up to just below the knees, so as not to slip on the skin, and lowers himself down into the chest of the giant.

And the giant's iced fingers clench.

All Misao has to do is make her way past the abandoned town—or follow the path behind the buildings, the one stoned-snaking through the pinion trees—to where the path and the road become one. One, she should walk, keep walking, keep dragging the sack of puke, and look for the turn-off, the denser wooden walk, and arrive.

The city of death—overrun, a slaughterfest seeping out to the desert, and beyond to the one road carved of octopus flesh.

So Misao crosses behind the town, lifts the sack, and darts down a back path so as not to be spotted by any of the night's denizens.

And Misao's chest burns from the whipping switch, but it's a burn she controls, an empowering stroke, not unlike the island sorcery of her youth. She ducks her head into the snow and darts off into the deepening woods.

The octopus brain tries to stick to her felt boots. She's light, though, and agile. Misao plucks a brain-bud and weaves around the pinions until she's sure she's found the path. A particularly thick stick, hardened white with crust, has been speared into the ground—Golo's doing, no doubt.

A sign of sorts to mark the way. The staff itself, a resonating instrument in its own right they used for a cemetery performance in the yellow spring. The choking fever of a gaggle of geese—a binaural collage. And the release of the goats. The pigs, how they blended. The possum, too.

Her shaman, the hermit—her Golo—how distraught he was by the death of his wife. And cut his hair. And wash his body in the brain of the beast, so he can be sharp again. His Ami, his all. And the mystery of her murderer and why he did not pursue, not that the police would help, no police to speak of on this messy mesa in the armpit of the world.

But here exists the possibility of an act.

To harness the nectar of the skull-split octopus—to move closer to the mystery of orgone, that was her purpose, as well— what pushed her body to unshackle her maidenhood, to carve and crawl and starve her way over ships and seas and cities and snakes. This mystery was why she listened to the flapper whore in the city who tried to bite, the whore who tried to shank her in the bathroom of brown porcelain and needles, and Misao opened her cracked lips and bit and spit, until the whore's face shone ragged strips of bloody rivers, unpeeled, incapacitated, frothing on the floor forevermore.

Thus, the revelation of Golo came to her.

Upon Misao's suggestion, they experimented with the properties of the leviathan's brain matter. The divine effects of the matter on the skin and the visions of memory and energy walls that followed. A psychophysical scalpel of rejuvenation.

But tonight was different. Golo's face was not the face of a graceful artist, it was a face of horror. Of violation.

And now Misao passes the last of the pinions and their spice, and, vomit sack still dragging, snow encircling, pushes her way up the stone path to Golo's shack in the woods.

A light is on and that should not be.

Earlier, Misao was the last one to leave. Golo had gone the long way through the town to spread the word of the performance.

She places the sack in the snow and slowly circles to the side of the shack. She pushes herself closer, fingers on the sill and peers into Golo's study. A single candle burns on his desk, its red wax bubbling out in a sloppy perimeter around the candle's base. She cocks her head to the doorway that leads to the main room, but cannot hear anyone or anything.

To the front porch, step by step.

To the locked door and what lies beyond.

The knob is coated in nectar. Misao licks her palm, tastes a sweet remembrance. And opens the door.

It is only a split second as if a still image appearing too quick to register, but registered and stored. A hallucination turned memory. The inability to unthink a happening. And the happening Misao sees and smells before her—chills skitter centipedes up her thighs—is framed in the doorway to Golo's study, the same study she just peeked into from the window outside.

A hulking man, cloaked in black, axe raised, back turned— basked in blood.

And he turns, looks directly at Misao with the mask of a grinning fox, a mask that resonates the sound of a gong rung, rung—

Misao blinks.

The candle sputters, burns.

She walks to the desk and snuffs the candle between two fingers. The room goes dark. Outside, the snow pattering at the window dizzies Misao, the sky streaking black and purple. She leans over the desk and breathes off the vision. But she's left the sack of puke outside in the snow.

Off to the east, she hears the caribou call. It starts as one, a trumpeting conjoining with the pastured goats. For a moment she lets herself become their whine, but the trumpeting morphs to a droning wail, a wall of motion. Misao drags the sack to the porch, kicks open the door and heaves it sloshing on the floor. She lights a lamp and another, tiptoeing around their living space to ignite every light in the shack, filled with the nightsong of the beasts. The thought they paint in her mind is of a young woman falling, falling backward to the wooden floor, palms up and empty, but she shuts her eyes.

It's Ami.

And there is no pain.

There is nothing but animal tongues clicking.

Inside the giant naked girl, Golo drops to a fleshy tunnel and it is not pitch dark on this side of the world.

Red illumination. The stench of a freshly opened body consumes him—it drifts, cartoons up his nose in blots. He shakes away the side visions the smell sparks: pigs and boars, frogs and viper's blood.

He winces—the crackles are near, a screech.

An owl hoots elsewhere down the tunnel—a caribou calls out in the far dark, through the snow.

Misao calls his name. She's on the shack's floor.

She calls his name and he is not there to come and help her out of the void.

The hole leading out of the woman sears and bubbles. Golo presses his palm to the fleshy dirt, licks his palm, intones a breath, but the smell, the smell is unlike the smells of his cupboard, his vat, his magic art. He wants more.

A temple bell's ping rings from the bowels of the giant.

Hands in pockets, Golo bows his head and steadies the fever inside him.

From his pockets, Golo pulls his whipping switch and woodblock.

The temple bell pings. Twice.

Golo rushes forward: to the crackle, the bubble, a mélange of purpling smells, blood-clouds popping across his eyeballs, and sensual moans peaking, dipping and repeat to—

Overpowering chants.

He enters a ritual chamber.

The belly of the giant naked girl, a hollowed out cavern lit round by thick red candles.

And three men in the center of a circle of masked naked women legs crossed in lotus: a caribou, a goat, a crane, a fox, an ape. The chanting swells from the men. One of them holds a circular gong, another, a temple bell. They strike in unison. And

Golo immediately bows, noticed as he is, by the men as they turn to face him, chant their spell within him. But Golo pushes against their tones, careful not to swallow whatever power they have created in their circle.

And more than this, for the image manifesting in Golo's mind is that of Ami. But the image cracks, his brain crackles, and a force from outside strikes the back of his head.

It's the fourth of the group, his bear-hands clubbing at Golo's skull.

And Golo claws, phlegms at the man—cannot hear, for the chants have swollen, the women and their animals—to rip off his face, but the face of the man is the visage of an octopus frowning, face dripping, one eye hanging, unblinking.

Golo swings the woodblock, cracks the mollusk man in that eye, but a meaty hand is already tightening its grip on his throat.

Golo's woodblock strikes the mollusk man's head, ever weakening. The beautiful hands of the masked women pull at this *hakama* and his suspenders, his coat and boot.

Golo struggles to regain control, but the dirt-flesh walls curve about him and the sound of the ritual fades with each grope and rip, the rip slowing as if each thread of his being tears to tiny clicks, miniature universes of holes, crags, gurgles, and he screams, wrenches at the arms that hold him. But Golo thrashes, can't swim from the pummel, the gropes, fingers tightening.

And Ami's hand webs to his—fox-faced, a brush of breath.

Somewhere, Misao falling.

The rushing of water freezes his lungs shut, cracks.

To inhale orgone.

The press of other bodies against his own.

Time passes fitfully, in blood.

Later.

Mallet to iron.

Oscillates to—

A temple bell pings, rings out through the cavern of the giant naked girl's innards. Strewn with flowers. The burning of stones to light the passages, little red holy rocks glowing like deformed

72

coals. They pulse. And come to a clearing of legs, to the womb chamber, to the stench of an abattoir—a death call.

Dorje traverses the tube, hunkering and slipping down into the high bloated sphere, fox mask in hand, black cloak swarming around him.

He slips his fingers into the folds of his robe, right hand wraps around a string of black beads and counts the beads.

Until he comes to the makeshift pyre: a clump of mollusk brain hammered flat to a paste, a bell and the blood, a stick of incense, red tip still glowing like those little rocks, holy smoke trailing a line of black swirls of intoxication. All placed within a wooden crate.

But the other brothers and sisters who came from afar, their bodies, are blitzed apart, torn into chunks and gobs, strewn across the sphere, staining the curved walls with splatters and splots.

Just a tick remains. An inner pendulum, steadying Dorje's trembling mind.

Someone has penetrated the veil, broken the trance.

Yet Kala has spoken and speaks now to the cycle of his desire, his retribution.

And breathe, Dorje—whose skin do you taste?

Channel the rag-dung to ring.

Let it fill, be full.

Dorje sits lotus position in the center of the filth. Spread fingers, palms up for the arcing of light to penetrate. And heal.

Float.

His bearded pale face tenses, slacks to the visage of a dead man, and those black eyes shut to a wall of inner blankness.

His scars glow.

And ticking.

Tick, shrinking frame.

Tick, spirit expanding.

To a fissure in the skull. A light.

Lips trilling the rag-dung.

Hovering.

Hover, night-snow gliding—the tumbling grace of a snowdrop afloat on the wind, ticking.

Tick, to a fleshy dot floating forward.

A choir of women.

Tick, encircle the violent one with the bloody hands. Of brothers.

And be lost—Dorje's body within girl-body levitating, a lotus in the center.

Right eye—snowing, snow freezing.

Left eye—opening what came before, to the chant and the pull, to the incredible smear of Golo's fury, his brutal action. The stench, too much for Dorje's left eye to bear, though he dare not look away lest he lose himself in an illusion. For the bodies of the others have been thrown around him, splattered and split with the flick of Golo's wrist. Fingers scoop eyeballs. Nails rake guts to threads. This man, now shivering his way to a shack in the woods.

This animal.

And ticking.

A strange box-like structure clouding the right.

The blood fills Dorje's left eye.

And when Dorje's body floats back to the ground—left eye blood-holed, gored—the axe is passed to his lap, placed within his hands from without. It rests in his robes.

"Thank you," Dorje says, and looking out at a point on the skin-walls of this body, he sees the structure hover before him.

Lest Golo enters orgone.

Lest orgone consumes him. Not for what he's taken tonight.

Yes, let death prevail like the burning city in the distant night.

Or the fire of a physician's pain.

Boots break snow, grind a machinist rhythm. Golo, dirtied, mind weary, clomps sloppy, holds up one arm to shield his face from the blizzard's spray. He's a grit-tooth hobbling mantra.

It's still night, pulsing night.

Exhale woods, skin, blood, and what lurks inside giants over hills with holes in their chests.

Golo is past the abandoned building of the night's ritual.

The orange ambience of the burning city beyond—a fiery splash of violence and body-slopped streets, a slop Golo knows he must harness, go beyond, for the orgone accumulator hums to him—disks, wires, electrodes, sine, triangle, loop. And even now traversing these vast frozen woods, he forges forward, shivering the thinned air. Taking breaths, he four-counts, repeats, struggles his way home—*in, two, three, four, out, two three, four.*

Yonder, bleating, haggard cawing as if the cold was a lost beast dying.

Eyes slit, crusting shut, he bats away branches, chops at ice webs, clomps on, breaks hanging blots of snow-mess, frozen leaves.

Just follow the wooden stakes, and the stakes are no one's fence, but well-built, nonetheless, half-buried in the ground. They serve as a wind-whipped path to Golo's shack.

And the caribou call, wolves lull among snake slithers.

The ground softens, hardens, brain-muscle shifting.

And the smell—a carrion musk surrounds.

Golo's mantra grows louder as he loses himself in the repetition of sacred words, swells him onward, palm to fence stake, weak palm to fence stake.

Step over frozen fur, a jetting of bone, pink seepage leaks dot here and there like tiny lights in the snow. A burbling pocket of octopus brain, manna for the sipping. Trembling, freezing, shivering thoughts of the blot he's suffered at the hands of those lurking within the giant naked girl, Golo wrenches a glob of pink and forces himself to chew enlightenment.

Swallow the flesh.

Chew divinity.

"Aum ramma salo kari," he says. "Or-gone aum ramma salo kari." He repeats these words, swallows, chokes and beats his chest, gags on through the snow, until his gags turn to octopus breaths.

Over another hill.

To the end.

Gunshots crackle in the distance.

Screams of the fallen. Or screams adrift on the wind from miles away. Or ancient snow-screams finding their way to the inside as Golo's ears have sealed shut from the cold.

And now, Golo gleams truth. The blockage was from the

others who ambushed him inside the giant girl's chest. A God Golo was not aware of, symbols and letters he could not read. The clenching in his chest. His jaw. Hands choking his throat. A constriction. Venom on his tongue.

For in that moment of violence, Golo was overcome with a furious hate—his wife's killers were among them.

Waiting for him as if destiny were a slice to the throat.

But he bled them out.

Each gory strand of their bodies, a click and a hum—breathe. The turning of sacrifice.

Shut your eyes and feel the sea—force the feeling to be, he thinks. Breathe snow-stuffed lungs to life. And rise, mollusk. Seep deeper. Breathe in gulps, gulp punishing air.

Golo stumbles on, lips dripping blood.

He's weaker now. "Don't collapse," he says to himself. "Soon, warm . . . and drink."

Yet the heady swill of Misao's piss elixir, a balm, a potion, still swishes inside him, bubbles over his mind as if her sacred waste were a trigger to heal him of his dead-Ami obsession.

And the discovery of Misao's natural medicine had been a blessing, the fruits of one of their psychosexual ritual actions.

The force of her heat had lit his heart to beat harder.

Ami would have been proud—proud of Golo, too, for the live action death-deed inside the giant naked girl.

But the mechanics of Misao's piss—thinks it may have something to do with Misao's relationship to the octopus, the elevation, perhaps. He doubts whether she understands.

He dares not ask for fear of knowing.

"Be aware, again." It's the rasp of his master, cloaked with the living face of Ami.

They hover before him, disappear before him.

Just a blink.

Golo curses. Misao's piss is not enough, though a balm, never enough, though a path to the other side, he needs more.

Needs orgone stimulation.

If only the truth were something to spew, chew, regurgitate.

His stomach grumbles.

And imagine—

There were more naked bodies within the girl's chest than Golo saw, thought he saw, through the smoke, if there was smoke. And he sees the scene now, cloaked in red waves:

Strawberry blonde fingernails to chest, raking blood. He is stripped. Thumbs drumming his neck, esophagus bruised, hollowed, licked—explodes blood. Tongues flickering the gorge. More sap. Sap turns nectar. To spread his body on the floor, pinned down and pummel, scream gurgles, pummel, suck gurgles. Flesh on flesh and wet on wet. Push flesh in folds. Smother. And the threat (whispered in his ear, licking lobes) to spill his guts open with a sharpened stone and smear his shaman blood on the corpse of a levitating pig as some form of curse—open mouth dripping, dipped, mouth pried and yanked, stuffed with pink.

There was a bell within the body and the hands of men and women or worse—gigantic beasts of the sea, crawling, clawing, insect-covered, flutters of his own madness. And that feeling in his mouth, the pain—a weakened jelly he fought to force down, but couldn't force out. A pain beyond the body.

The pain of helplessness.

Those were not soft hands, supple hands that help. They were death-hands, eager.

Certainly the vision was worse.

He could no longer tell.

In that moment: overcome with horror, Golo struck, kept striking: bite, lash, punch, tear, release. The sounds of the others' death-gore warped to a hollow fuel, a gurgling from afar as if his ears were no longer a part of his body, but somewhere miles away, into the void.

Closer now to warmth: a cup of boiled cola extract and ginger, crust of bread, liver bits, pig bits.

He walks in crouched steps, coat tucked to his chin. To the door of his shack.

"Misao," he calls out, stuttering to the slatted porch. He has forgotten the cries of the animals, though their chanting melts to a din over fresh thunder.

And more snow to bury him, whips up around him.

Under staff or lute—thunder.

Mallet to iron—the rumbling earth.

Golo's legs stiffen in the snow. He drops and crawls, the front door of his shack, so close. Paws his way home. And yet, he is overcome by the sour smell of the inside of the giant naked girl: legs spread, dirty tongues, blood. Enough for him to see out of the edge of his blinking eyeballs, a swirling purple circle in the wild night sky shrinking.

And thunder, more thunder.

The door opens with a loud boom.

Golo's blood-iced hand trembles outward toward the opening, fingers sliced hard as if the octopus brain trickle he swallowed has tingled to the nerves of his very being.

Golo shudders, arm trembling, vision blotting black spots.

And she's there, standing, alive.

Misao—his shamanic savior—doused olive-drab in the candle light. Her ritual robe drapes in waves and obi sash fastened across her thin waist. A steel spike to hold up her hair so it fans out above and behind her back, beautiful. She's radiant. "Golo," she says. Thunder blitzes the sky and the purple contracts, spit spirals of light blue currents in tangles. "What is—where did you disappear to?"

She pulls him to the shack's warmth, his stiffened legs limp in the snow, *hakama* bloodied and battered, and her touch is like a creamy blur, how he sinks to the floor, hears insects croak whirlwinds of peace from her breasts, and mouth open, he waits for nectar.

For all has gone soggy.

Pulled to the main room, face up, mind melting, shivering, she begins the healing operation.

Misao squats over Golo and pulls up at her robe, rubs herself across his face, souping him wet with her pelt while humming, and Golo mumbles his mantra: "Aum ramma salo kari. Orgone aum ramma salo kari." But the crackling fire deeper inside the shack—something sharp burbling from a small pot—causes his eyes to sting. And Misao's flush bud drips nectar.

The hot drip streams.

To flow a wave of honey down his throat. And drink: heal the weak, expel the poison.

To show Golo where *she's* been—flat on her back, animal vision suffered. A cloaked man of blood. A man of the axe.

What she's seen—the beasts, the cries.

Or the mystery that has been summoned to the shack—a present, perhaps, for Golo's purpose.

A specter of lucidity.

Drink.

From tip to toe.

Phase Two: Complete

Upon stirring from his meditation, Dorje stalks his way to the edge of the city.

He leaves the giant naked girl where she had fallen in the snow, her flesh to become rotting nutrients for the frozen octopus landscape.

And the bodies inside.

The ruined pyre.

Dorje weeps, kicks at a clot of ice forming over the girl's side. "May you be a haven to those who have lost," he says. "May animals sing in your tunnels."

Or beasts who stalk the void.

Thus, Dorje sets out.

As an adept of the New Golden Dawn, he would need to utilize Ukko, the cavernous seer, a man who could grant a wordless way into the nature of his journey, the help he sought.

Help to vaporize Golo.

At least, he thinks, Ukko could guide—elevate. Dorje needed a guide.

That was not going to be an easy task.

Orgone, no matter what form it manifested or was formed into, posed a risk the New Golden Dawn were just beginning to manipulate.

Its essence was valuable.

And Dorje had known the end of Ami—the original orgonotic shaman. Her death-energy had served his brothers and sisters well, served his own masters with psychic freedom.

Some shamans, he was told by others who came before him,

must be ceased by any means necessary—when instructed by means of the proper channels, for the sake of order. For necessary power shifts to occur.

Ami's channel was the end of his axe.

Other than that, she meant nothing to Dorje. Just a body.

The order had been passed to Dorje like how the elders of the secret commune in days long gone sent him to the outlying areas—zones of unpredictability—in search of rare unguents, gems, alchemical spices, limbs, and guts until the Day of the Homunculus buried the elders' commune in a flurry of dust and bone-salt, death and dirt. That was years past.

The brothers and sister of the New Golden Dawn came in their robes and spells, so they said it to be, on horseback and pig-head skin masks, in ancient jeeps with spiked tires dragging the head of the Homunculus behind them.

Dorje surrendered to their strength.

Now, Dorje stands hunched at a burned-out restaurant, an awful building with a dilapidated burnt orange, slatted roof, broken windows and splattered brick, overturned tables inside like fallen chess pieces of antiquity. Something behind the counter, as he hovers in front of the building, slithers to silent rest with each glass-crunching step Dorje takes.

Behind him, the vast unfolding of the mesa, snow-covered doom, tinged purple and black streaks.

"For the light," he mutters, "for the heart, for the unspeakable spirit of Horus," reaching up to his shoulder, feeling the cold sting of his axe. He smells feces and sour blood waft on the icy wind.

Gunshots blare beyond.

Dorje dares not wonder. "No time like the present," he says.

He hauls back, kicks open the restaurant's front door, sends it crashing off its hinges. He swings the axe around, unhooks it from his makeshift straps. In case, he thinks, wondering about that slither, wondering who or what monstrosity remained in the dark rubble of the restaurant.

The stench of rotten noodles.

Eggs.

Fortuneless cookie piles.

And flies, bodies of them swarming over a goopy body—just a pool of slop on the floor.

Below him, the world itself rumbles for a moment, growls. It is slight and, in that moment, Dorje wonders if it's just his heart-patters in the dark. Or his feet wanting to flee far, far away from this city, this mesa, and back to the comfort of his dojo. He has not yet grown used to the sensation of hunting atop a gigantic frozen octopus, doesn't like it much either, and save for the purpose of the ritual power it apparently grants, the reason him and his New Golden Dawn brothers and sisters set out to the mountain in the first place—Ceremony of Orgonotic Mining—he prefers his sea level lifestyle: the temple silence, the cherry blossoms, the southern fields and the majesty of southern women.

Dorje cranes his head to see better in the dark folds of the battered restaurant. A scuttling sound hits his ears from the back. Or clawing up a wall, around paintings. The ceiling creaks. And yes, there is a door, a faint backlit rectangle, edges of green light. It's the door he knows he needs to enter. He steps over fallen tables, broken chairs. An armored car clunks by outside. More gunshots from the depths of the city.

Orange shadows jump, dance across the restaurant's exterior.

"What is this place?" Dorje says to himself. "Pray I'll live to leave it."

And that scuttling sound, more a rattle than a scuttle, scrapes from behind the door in the back. Dorje recalls the scuttle of Favian and Cross, the battlefield left barren and bloodied before he burned their bodies. He wept at the smell.

It was the smell of regretful indifference, of cowardice.

But before Dorje can react, a chain whips out from that door in the back and wraps around his throat, tightens, pinching his air, gulping up his heart to stop, and dropping him to his knees.

"Ukko—no," Dorje chokes, but it's too late for him. The chain is yanked taut by strong hands and Dorje is pulled to the floor, heaved, dragged atop broken glass shards, shit-stained linoleum tiles, animal innards, bones.

"Ukko—it's—stop," he gurgles. "Dorje."

Two leathered hands feed and pull the chain shorter, shorter,

ORGONE

skidding Dorje across the floor, closer to the monster in charge. A boot to Dorje's shoulder kicks him onto his back. His purpled grimace stares up at a man with no skin covering his face—pure bloody muscle and lidless eyeballs, nose holes minus the nostrils, and a grinning lipless mouth. The man speaks tersely, his white button down dress shirt, black slacks, black shoes not a match for the destroyed decor of the Chinese restaurant: "Dorje, the sneaking backbone of night visitations," Ukko says. "You should be more than careful, young man, or you'll end up dead, head wrenched from your body like tearing the bud from a stalk of shit." And as Ukko speaks, he loosens the chain wrapped tight around Dorje's neck.

Dorje wrenches on the chain, his neck already cut from the chain's jagged alteration.

"Could have killed me," Dorje says.

"But didn't."

"Should have known."

"Didn't know you were coming all this way."

"To wake you up," Dorje says.

Ukko drops the chain, reaches into his pants pocket. "Must be urgent then," he says, pulling out a packet of old rolled tobacco. "Or maybe you're already a dead man?"

"Name's Golo—common mesa dweller, but he's an orgone shaman."

"Name's not familiar," Ukko says, lighting a cigarette. "Nor does it have to—"

"Can you tap?"

"It's possible."

"What do you want?"

"You can owe me," he says, smiling rotten.

Ukko would rather not think about how, something too much to handle on a night of this significance.

"Some taps are more," Ukko says, "shall we say, *intense,* than others."

"I underestimated him—mined his apprentice, though."

Ukko releases a fog of sharp cigarette smoke, turns and enters the back room.

And Dorje, on his feet, looks out into the dark: the snow, the glowing death, and how the hard floor of the Chinese restaurant feels harder, more stable, on the lopped head of an octopus. He touches his thumb to his forehead and whispers to himself, eyes closed, and slides his thumb down to his heart.

A harsh white light burns his eyes. Ukko has slipped on a white laboratory coat, a pair of black-rimmed glasses, and a surgical face mask.

For a micro-second, the room blips green, swells.

Dorje swallows and enters, unsure if he'll ever exit again.

A candle for each corner—red wax stumps melting.

The vat bubbles, has been stirred by a juniper branch, a fire crackling underneath.

Golo wipes his mouth, swallows the last of the stewed pig entrails prepared by Misao. He burps, spits a shred of gut on the floor.

Misao tells him everything she recalls.

The only answer Golo gives: "Some kind of spell—a premonition of your death. Or mine."

She shakes her head, running her hand across her neck and down the front of her robe.

When Misao awoke on the floor of the shack, she felt her body become lighter, mouth parched, and a crushing weight on the back of her head.

Was there a man who had entered the shack?

Had she been attacked?

Why doesn't she remember what happened?

So Misao bathed in the vomit of Golo's performance, submerged herself in a peculiar concoction and sank, breath held, release, clench. This was Golo's instruction, for he added the unknown contents of one of his blood-buckets he keeps sealed under the house.

And he blessed her forehead.

And he kept her there. At peace.

But the present. She said she had prepared a present. She would not say, unsure if what she had prepared was still among them and not just a figment of her imagination.

The present Misao offers to show Golo is in his shed behind the shack. She warns him of what he might see and when he asks her "How?" or "Who?" or "What magic she's wrought?" she replies with: "The visitation occurred when I awoke, wandering outside the shack."

"What is this about?"

"It must be about you," she says. "I believe you somehow summoned this to be—like it's for you, Golo."

Golo buttons his coat and trudges out to the shack, turning back, says, "Boil me a cup of the vomit—if this is as heady as you speak of it."

And he stands outside—*in, two, three, four, out, two, three, four*—still slightly shaking from the night's barrage of happenings. He admits defeat in terms of the effect of the performance at the abandoned building—the sounds and smells of their psychophysical training. He had rehearsed, but the interference left him helpless.

Once the possession begins, there is no turning back.

He unlatches the shed lock and swings the door open to an inner swirl of insect chirps, swirling violins, and the underpinning rumble of his mind coming suddenly unhinged. The sight throws him backward, but he remains standing. And his skull tingles, pumps. An oscillating wave that destroys his perception of the outside world.

He stands haunted, staring at the figure of the long dead father of orgonotic therapy, the dead, yet not so dead—Wilhelm Reich.

He hears the back door to the shack creak open. Misao crosses her arms. "He is here for you," she says. "Still here, no doubt, by your shrieks. And the serum is boiled."

"For me?" Golo says, staring at Reich, but speaking to himself.

Golo had studied Reich's breath work while at the Acrid Temple. His master kept a vast collection of books in the dojo's second basement. Reich's hermetic texts on breathing ranked among his master's most prized troves. And Golo had studied them all—mirror work, the de-armoring of the body, character analysis, the bioelectrical energy of sex, the orgasm—and orgone, the root of Reich's research. The diving board for the Acrid Temple's guiding principles.

Indeed, Golo spent years of lotus breath work, orgone concentration, and summoning actions. His master revealed the Fourth Way, the Seven-Headed Release Pose, as well as Orgone Combat Techniques for Mental Stimulation.

But to have Wilhelm Reich standing before him was too much to comprehend. Golo and Misao were not versed in enfleshment magic.

Their psychophysical exercises aimed to sharpen, not harm. Yet,given this, Golo still could not explain the energy he had unleashed inside the chest of the giant naked girl.

Reich coughs, hits his chest to clear phlegm.

Golo mutters his mantra quickly.

"You called upon me," Reich says, graveled voice, deep yet soothing, accented and strong, stepping forward. He wears a flannel hunting jacket, black wool pants, a wool sweater underneath. His hair sprouts electric waves around his head and his pudgy face pulsates even in the single-bulb darkness of the shed. "And we have work to do—ages to explain this anomaly of circumstance."

"But how—where did you come from?"

"Heaven and Earth, Horatio," Reich says. "And beyond, I would assume."

"Beyond," Golo says, awe-struck, head still rumbling, pierced and woozy.

"I'll show you, seems to be the way," Reich says. "We haven't much time."

"Time?" Golo says.

"The accumulator," Reich says, but his right hand fades in the green light, reappears. Reich and Golo look at each other and in that moment Golo realizes it was, somehow, the simultaneity of his and Misao's mental connection that tapped Reich to materialize. But how is that possible with two minds? Materializations were meant to be triadic.

Unless the giant naked girl's chest created some kind of amplification.

Or the animals.

Or the octopus brain, itself.

And across a vast plain of brain-tinged snow, flame-drenched buildings charred and pluming smoke to the east and north, within the back room of a dilapidated restaurant, Dorje lies prone, strapped to a gurney under harsh fluorescent neon bulbs. The room is a linoleum-tiled mess of odd medical gadgets—broken metal, mechanical contraptions gutted, wire piles—and blood-soaked smocks draped over workbenches: hammers, wrenches, scalpels, razor blades. A windowless room.

Yellowed walls.

It is a night to Transcend.

Ukko, so he says or has been called by the New Golden Dawn, is a doctor of psychoneurotics. Dorje was introduced to Ukko months back at one of the New Golden Dawn's tantric desert ceremonies, an all-night affair beyond the mountain snow, near the Dawn's encampment, near the bases and huts, just miles from where the squid infestation washed on the beach in bloody humps, bled the sand unwalkable.

A dead zone of nomads.

A dirty mess of a desert radiation.

And Dorje worries. He worries the procedure he's about to undergo might leave him somehow lesser the man, somehow deader the man. He watches Ukko furiously pen some message in the corner, scribbles letters into a black notebook and laugh. The man's laugh is like the cackle of a nightmare. Dorje's heard that laugh before. And Dorje worries what he will confront when the procedure begins. Not having undertaken the procedure in the past makes him wary. In fact, everything about Ukko makes him wary. But he's here to equip himself for the murder-journey to come, for a way to penetrate Golo's universe from the inside of his own mind, and transfer whatever power he possesses back to himself—and from Dorje to the New Golden Dawn orgone shall rein.

Yes, he thinks, to the future of orgonotics.

And in the process, he'll kill Golo for what he did. He'll kill the woman Golo keeps by his side, too.

The Ami experience all over again, only bloodier.

Only better.

It is true she conjured Dorje to Golo's shack only hours before during his walking meditation. He knows she is not to be undervalued.

And she has seen the murder.

An animal priestess of the highest order.

"We're ready then, are we?" Ukko says. He stretches a pair of dirty brown plastic gloves over his skinny fingers.

Dorje nods and adjusts himself on the gurney.

"First time is the best," Ukko says. "Take off your clothes and we proceed."

Dorje sits up. "For what purpose?"

"To receive your new body."

A new body. Dorje didn't know about this part of the procedure, but was in no position to argue and it was too late to turn back. The brothers and sisters have been slaughtered by the man they were set out to study—slaughtered by Golo. He needed to get to the inside as soon as possible. Ukko was his key.

The first patch to left temple.

The second patch to right.

Three clips to the skin over central cortex.

Clamp the spine.

Syringe the spinal cord—let the patient sleep.

Let all sleep and be sleepy, awake to the other side.

But Dorje, now strapped to a gurney, naked and shivering, was not going under smoothly. There was a hate festering across his body, the likes of which Ukko had not seen.

Not that that was a surprise.

Tapping a patient's brain to ether always came with some kind of unintended consequence. Every patient was different—unique, beautiful.

Ukko palmed a hunting knife and slid it across Dorje's forehead. By now, Dorje would not be able to feel the pain, overcome as he surely was by other forms of unpleasant grandeur. So, Ukko reached behind him and pulled out two tabs connected to red wires. He carefully inserted both tabs under Dorje's forehead, so they rested comfortably on his skull, on the outside of his brain. Ukko then reached under the gurney and switched on a small metallic box. He turned a dial on the box and waited for it to warm up. A needle in the center of the box flickered back and forth, settling in the middle. Ukko cranked the dial.

Something rattled outside his back room laboratory.

"Not now," Ukko says. "Always in the middle . . . "

Breathe—

Fingers twitch—curl and sag.

Dorje's body stops shivering, goes limp. Ukko smiles, strokes Dorje's head.

But the sound from the restaurant persists, pushes into Ukko's eardrums—*snap, snap, snap*—such that, breaking the tradition of how these things are normally done, he sets the metallic box's dial to its highest amplification, places it beside Dorje's body, and, with hunting knife in hand, unbolts the lock to the door, forging out to handle whatever critter needs handling at this hour of the night.

In the destroyed dining area of the restaurant, Ukko fails to see Dorje's limp hand twitch again, twitch harder fast, suddenly consumed by a shell of purple electric waves. Dorje fails to see that purple electricity completely consume Dorje's face.

Under the sedation of the tapping medication, Dorje does not scream.

From the outside, Dorje's body is being existentially mutilated.

Breathe—

Follow the purple (swelling, deepening, intensifying) under fluttering eyelids and up into his brain-chasm, past the vertex where it sparks, to where twin hemispheres meet the horizon of outer mind.

And there, one will find the body of Dorje.

But it is not fully Dorje.

Something grows.

Brain-nectar drips of him.

Becomes—

It's all too odd for Golo. He shivers, tastes pink, clears his throat. The white-haired wraith, the father of orgonotics stands before him—Wilhelm Reich, a dead man risen. Or the semblance of him. Flesh sorcery.

There's something not right about Reich's visage, a pale radiance. A fake fleshiness bordering on a substance other than skin surrounds his body.

To touch, knead, sever a false history.

"Come, sit," Golo says, arms folded tight across his chest, stepping backward toward the shack before he even knows he's moving. "Mr. Reich—our traveler, our savior."

And when Reich speaks—a mumbled garble of choppy static oscillations ring—it's his mouth Golo peers into, how that mouth is a pitch black oval of nothing, a toothless abyss between the lips.

A rumble. More gunshots pitter from afar.

The three of them hover as strangers for a moment, triangulated toward each other, unable to comprehend. Not knowing what to say.

"Please, Doctor," Misao says. "We are eager to—"

"Orgone," Golo says.

But Reich places his index finger to his lips and blows a shush to cease the talking. His mouth smoothly moves from a pursed tightness to a toothless laughter of static warbles. The sound sends shivers over Golo's back, until the laughter cuts off.

Golo squints, remains skeptical, though he doesn't doubt—can't not admit—the reality of the man standing before him. So lifelike and thick. Blood under skin. Too glimmering, though, as if his insides were stuffed: gears, fluff, sky. Reich laughs again, more maniacal.

Golo waits for the laughter to stop, hearing it squelch itself within the falling snow, the vast distances of the mollusk mesa. "What then?" Golo says. "What else is there, other than orgone?"

Reich nods, turns to the shed and extends his arm, fingers outstretched like an ancient showman gesturing for the cage to open, to unleash tigers, lions into the meat-pit. He's gesturing toward the shed. His fingers shake.

"It can't be—you came from there, my shed?" Golo says. "Misao, did you . . . " he tries to say, but his voice trails. For he knows what lies on the other side of that old wooden shed door. Yet there is magic in Reich's gesture. For in that moment of Reich's gesture, Golo is aware—an awareness pressed into him from Reich's inner being—of what Reich was doing in the shed. Maybe he has been there for days, weeks upon weeks. A time of Immateriality—the sacred zone. Golo has read about such conjurations. A materialized being operating not within the realm of the ordinary, but the supernatural. Beyond time. And of course, if the conjuration had been that strong, then surely there would be more secrets to reveal. Perhaps there are hundreds of Reichs roaming the countryside.

The ground tremors, blurring Golo's vision. It doesn't matter. This world could burn, melt to a slab of nose-lard and Golo wouldn't budge, for, indeed, he knows the other side is nearer than it's ever been before.

He wants to enter the shed, is ready to enter the other side.

Whatever project Reich has brewed.

And maybe, he thinks he can find Ami on the other side, too.

Reich's head snaps toward Golo—jaw clicks, clicks opens—startling Misao, who counts spells on her fingers, trying to piece together the proper preparatory materials for orgone sharpening if the need arises to retaliate or flee. Or something stronger, transformative. She won't say. But her wavering mind is still a whirl of where Golo must have been: the blood splatters on his *hakama*, skin stench, the fear and the violence wafting off his skin as he ate his dinner in a blind rage, calm silence, earlier in the evening, unblinking. She's worried for the safety of their souls. Realms unfathomable. In what he won't tell her. She's worried whatever murderer she knows cursed her with a hallucinated visitation earlier in the night will be back for more—at least in her mind. That figure will return, spill her blood in the snow.

When Reich speaks, Golo and Misao know they are supposed to understand the significance of his words. What he teaches, has taught from Old Europe to this New America: bioenergy, orgone therapy, character analysis, armoring, liberation, body healing. The possibility of hope. They can't understand him, though, ears craned to listen. A blast. Again, his voice sparks a radio signal out of focus, a blur of warped bass glitches and distorted blares at once close and far as if from a control tower in the city. But he goes on and on, orating nothing but static. The message lost. His brow tightens, arms flail. And the speech is heightened, shifting the sounds to an orchestra of blaring noise bending to a hiss.

Hiss shifting, fades to a shut mouth.

And silence.

Reich shakes his head in disapproval, and grandly pulls open the shed door, revealing the enigma of a human-sized metal box placed neatly in the center of the shed.

He reveals an orgone accumulator.

The accumulator's door creaks open.

And it's a thing of wonder.

Of psychic divinity.

Golo draws a quick breath, boot-steps feverishly to the shed door, past Reich and his sour stench, to the inside of the shed. When Golo enters the shed, he finds the space feels larger than normal as if the walls had been extended by meters wide—wider than that—and the ceiling, too. And the orgone accumulator beckons before him as a foreign obelisk, so distant, yet something he would have created by his own mind. He hears Misao's soft feet slide into the shed. She gasps when she sees the accumulator.

It's brilliant. A simple mystical brilliance.

Golo is already at the device, its metallic door open, calling for him to come and sit. The only light within the shed is the dull blue moon light above in the sky, one that flickers as the snow blots out its faint luminescence.

An electric light burns on above, Misao's finger on the switch. And indeed, the shed is larger on the inside as if the accumulator had pushed the entire room back, bending space so the shelves of jars, rusty tools, and piles of gory powder Golo had amassed for his rituals were somehow pressed neatly further.

Up close, Golo observes the alternating materials that compose the accumulator's edges. He pulls back to consult with Reich, but Reich did not enter the shed and is still outside. Even if he were, Golo wouldn't be able to communicate his joy to this strange man of this very strange night. He reaches his hand in to touch the materials. Fingers on metal. Slide fingers and touch a layer of hardened octopus brain. Seven layers deep. Yes, it is true.

He didn't know it was possible to solidify the substance, had not thought to do such a thing, but he was not the Doctor, nor the architect. And still, he bites his own lip to reassure himself he is not dreaming. That this is really happening.

And it is.

Inside the accumulator, the metal layer reflects silver and a metal chair has been placed in the center. The entire box that encloses the accumulator is just larger than Golo himself when seated. And he touches the accumulator like a mad scientist in love with his creation. With longing. "Reich," he says, eyes still fastened to the box, glowing from the potential of what comes next. "This is an incredible—we can't waste anymore time, we, just—Misao, did you—?"

She's smiling in wonder at the accumulator, can hear its hum like a thick fog calling out to her. Outside, an animal whines and mewls in the far distance. And she blinks away the image of a giant naked dead girl frozen in the snow. She touches Golo on the shoulder and he stands to face her. "It's your time," she says.

"How did he . . . ?"

"There's a third, Golo."

"So it wasn't a hallucination."

She holds his hand. "He's coming to kill you in there."

"You can't kill orgone," Golo says. "It becomes Other."

"There are tortures worse than becoming a corpse."

"I will not die, Misao." His skin is feverish, palm suddenly clammy. "Orgone breeds life—a new life—and chance for liberation. It's all we have now." But he does not move to touch her, to hold her or kiss her on the lips. "This is the way it has to be." He's looking over her shoulder, struggling to see Reich still out in the snow, but the light in the shed burns to its fullest illumination and the outside is a black hole, a thick dark, like the inside of Reich's mouth. "And any tortures, here or elsewhere, worse than death are worth whatever psychophysical mysteries this accumulator holds."

But Misao clenches her fist. She doesn't believe him.

The screams of a suffering man belch out from his teeth to the shit-sucking grin of the man who strapped him down.

A dilapidated restaurant on the edge of town.

Ukko flips a switch. Turn knob to maximum penetration. Mind infiltration. A panel lights up. A backroom laboratory gone neon streaks: green lights, electric pulse on the temples, a body with skin melting, emptying arcs of blood. Liquid skin revival. Ukko reaches into his lab coat pocket, lights a blood-stained cigarette.

The skin on his own face has been sucked off by years of psychophysical experiments, perversions—time ill-spent in the radiation zones. Too many desert rituals to count. And now, this neophyte on the table.

Watch his muscles burn.

Teeth grind.

The tapping procedure is an orchestra of pain unfolding. Better than the last four, Ukko thinks, not looking to the storage closet—the buckets. The pails and bags. He's learned since then how to use the outer shell to seep inwards and beyond like a portal. But it's never the same trip for the participant—deadly fun for Ukko.

A final twist of a palm-sized blue knob and the pressure's been set. Rarely does the participant awaken in the middle of a tapping session such as this one, but he can never be sure. For now, though, he listens to the buzz of the electric lights streaming the ceiling. Glitching.

Ukko fails to witness the transformation.

The lights flicker as Dorje's body mutates on the table from human to monstrous mass of skin and eyes, bones, innards and a heart rapid and racing.

Ukko fiddles with coins in his pocket, lost in thought—the flickering lights—and sucks the smoke low into his lungs, breathes out a cloud, coughs, clears his throat, remains turned away from the thrashing monstrosity that is now Dorje; Dorje has become Other.

Dorje's eyes are sealed shut, fleshed over, unseeing the outside and the rage bubbling up from his guts. The initial blast of Ukko's electric concoction drilled his entire body in a blinding splurt of horrifying pain. The final image in his imagination as the mad doctor fiddled with buttons, cables, electrodes, blue wires, was the slaughterhouse scene inside the giant naked girl. For a brief instance Dorje pieced his image of Golo into the imagined scene, how it must have taken place, and tried to reassemble the chaos to a more profitable outcome of Golo as the ritualized body, held down by force, torn apart by savage hands for the sake of the New Golden Dawn. The orgone energy seeping from his dying body, being sucked into the souls of Dorje's brothers and sisters. The rancid air swirled with violins, bells, flutes and drums. The sound of rejoicing.

For in that image of Golo, with the introduction of the awful pain-waves sent by Ukko in the lab, the entire image conjured by Dorje's mind, changed for the worst.

A snapping jaw enflamed. Blood. Yellow teeth grit, grinding, mashing skin to—

Veins spilled open, splashing. A gush of guts.

The sisters flayed by skinny fingers.

The brothers encircled by the feeling of tangled viscera.

And the sound of the violins, the bells, the flutes, drums switch to a harsh chasm of noise. A shock of distortion: scrapes, shreds, cackles, roars of mutilation.

The blur of Dorje's mind slips into the flow from Ukko's tapping experiment.

Dorje doesn't grasp the shift, but the image in his mind is shielded by the noise as if the curtain were an amplification system to the Void.

The pain does not permit thought, blots it to blank space.

Nor does Dorje realize the gruesome twists of his new body.

But it doesn't matter to him, for the intense mind-blurring pain is an exit and a corridor.

To a naked body, shrouded in black space.

Filled with a heavy silence, thick tundra.

And a tiny blip of bright white. The distance, spinning.

Dorje looks to his hand, but it is liquid and clear. He gropes toward the tiny blip, can't yet move.

The blip shifts deep red.

And the blip shoots across the darkness toward Dorje too quickly for him to grasp the oncoming horror.

Outside the shed, Misao scans the dark for Reich. Wolves call from beyond and suddenly something crashes inside Golo's humble shack. She patters to the back door to check.

She touches the door handle, stops, presses her ear to the door. The smell of sliced meat boiling. Inhale. A heavy shuffle and that static garble. Reich's voice, she thinks. But within the sounds and the smells, with her ear to the door, she feels a distinct unease about entering. Something is not right.

And Reich is not on the inside.

She turns the handle. Quietly.

Behind her, back in the shed, Golo kneels *seiza* style as if preparing himself for a tea ceremony. His eyes are shut and if one could pry open his eyelids, one would find those eyes completely rolled back into his cranium. Eyes to the vertex. Scanning his inner light, gripping at the edges of his internal vision. He mouths his mantra, unbuttons his coat in deliberate gestures. Rigid hands shivering. Fingers straight. And underneath, his naked chest, still stained octopus-pink and his suspender straps black and bloodstained.

He throws off the coat. It reminds him of his time in the city. The Bullet Era. Fire and Misery.

He repeats the mantra, turns to face the accumulator, does not shut his eyes as he invokes stillness. The box is a thing of beauty. Mystery par excellence. Golo has heard stories from the lower chambers—tales etched in blood—of those who disappeared within its orgone power.

And he looks down at his own hands, stained in octopus matter as they are. It makes him think that what if perhaps he, himself and his madness, built the accumulator and just doesn't remember? No, that can't be possible. And where was Reich when Ami was murdered? More importantly, how was Reich possible without being directly summoned? He hisses out the end of his mantra and blinks three times to snap himself from his mind-wandering trance.

Golo stands and bows before the orgone accumulator. Of course, Misao has wandered off. He would like her to be here for this, to ensure nothing goes wrong, but something else inside him is pushing him to enter, to begin, to continue whatever psychophysical journey was already in progress. And perhaps he, too, would be healed from the misery of violence and his wife's slaughter. Perhaps, he would be healed from the trauma of the city. Perhaps, he would disappear into the folds of the Void, become a speck of the universe, an element. And that, he had come to think, would not be such a bad thing.

He enters the orgone accumulator and shuts the door, locks it from the inside. He sits on the chair, the metal cold against his back.

Breathe, hear breath rattle, wheeze.

Focus on the unending breath, on breathing.

The inside of the orgone accumulator is, at first, an intense darkness. Even with his eyes shut, the darkness of the accumulator presses against his eyeballs.

He feels weighted.

Shut eyes staring.

Until the black turns a wicked pink bending to touch blue, thick like liquid blue.

Golo folds his hands over his lap, back of his right hand into his left palm. He tries to voice the mantra, but no sound comes out of his mouth, and the silence grows heavier, so heavy he doesn't notice the rumble outside the accumulator, for he is All and Everything in blue waves, until—

The disintegration of his body, a lifting.

Skin melting upward and outward.

The box of blue orgone radiating into his body.

The heat of his body flames under skin from toe to skull.

Golo's lungs pulsate from the blast of blue orgone.

He can't scream, mouth ripped open.

There is no sound. His open mouth becomes a ragged bloody channel for the orgone to enter. And it enters through his nose and his ears like smoke, permeates through the invisible pores in his skin.

Teeth turn goo.

But inside Golo, there is nothing but the sensation of a light lifting to wonder, a suspension in blue ecstasy.

When Misao dashes into the shed, sees the blue light rimming the edges of the orgone accumulator, she gasps, rushes closer. She slides open a small square window for observational purposes.

She screams.

The window is splattered in Golo's blood.

Dorje comes to, fully clothed and refreshed, though wispy, body of light, like he could lift off the ground if he merely willed himself to do so. He's standing on a great, vast plain of sheer blackness. If he looks hard enough, he can just make out great obsidian shapes. Mountains with their jagged ridges. In front of him, the ground is level and smooth. Marble. A light emanates over this space where he finds himself and a kind of vignette of a simple wooden table, a wooden chair, and an equally wooden door are feet away from him. And perhaps he is on a stage. He looks again to the darkness, but now he sees neither mountainous form or otherwise, just a simple unending black shield.

He smells of pickled hearts, fermented ginger.

Dorje does not remember being strapped to the table, nor Ukko, the sadist. He touches his body in feverish gropes, rubs his eyes.

Static blackens, cuts his vision.

When he opens his eyes, a crackly projection of Golo sits at the wooden table. Dorje screams, stumbles back. The door opens and Ami, very much alive, yet crackling in static bursts like Golo, stands before her lover. She's pristine. Neither Golo nor Ami take notice of Dorje. Neither of them, he immediately thinks, are really here. And he's noticed that the blackness hovering around him and the odd vignette is moving like thick liquid in a swirling pattern of black.

Ami steps to her lover, wraps her arms around his neck. He's bent over that table writing, though he doesn't hold a pen, nor is there paper laid out before him. "What is this?" Dorje says. "Some kind of mockery?" He laughs, but the laughter doesn't help and the performers cannot see him. The blackness swirls faster and he feels it going to his head. The dizzy rush of disorientation—hot flashes, red spots in her eyes. And breathe. Regain control.

He walks to the scene, stands opposite the table and crouches. Ami whispers into Golo's ear, causing Golo to raise his head and take note. A smile cracks across his face and he looks up at his wife. He is about to speak—

Pause.

They freeze.

Their images crackle and fizz, but the projection is still vivid. Dorje stares, mouth agape, but the horror sinks in. This moment of stillness is the moment he slaughtered Ami. It was this pose and all he has to do is move in behind her, raise his axe and hammer it down into her skull, explode her skull to bits. Repeat. But Dorje is alone in this space. And he doesn't have his axe. He doesn't remember when he had it.

He leans over the table, close enough to Golo's face to smell the tape-like static smell of his synthetic visage. Suddenly, Dorje snaps out an arm to Golo's throat, but his hand goes right through the holographic image. Though, now, Golo's eyes lower from his lover's gaze and affix themselves on Dorje, who jolts back at those eyes.

What they hold.

What they reflect.

For pinging off Golo's eyes is the inside of the giant naked dead girl.

Misao gasps, appalled, rushes forward to pry open the door to the accumulator. She cannot. The door won't budge, pink brain-juice seeping out from the edges, sealing the door to the frame. A low buzz like the sound of power lines sings out from inside the accumulator. She wrenches, pounds on the door, screams Golo's name, but he does not reply.

She darts out of the shed, needs to find Reich.

The world outside the shed is still save for the sound of her own labored breath. Then, she spots him.

Reich is not in the shack. Reich has wandered to the hill to the west of their house; through the snow, she sees his body levitating horizontally several feet above the ground, his body surrounded by dark blue waves, neon strings of electricity encircling him.

Binding him to the air.

Back to the shack, Misao shoves open the back door, knocks over Golo's bowl of half-eaten pig bits, and rushes to the vat.

It has come to this, she decides. To the fringe.

She picks up a jar of rooster blood, pours it into the bubbling mixture, and intones an elaborate prayer, her arms extended high above her head. Muscles clench. She shoves her head into the vat and drinks, vomits, drinks, cries, and drinks more, until her entire head is drenched in blood, puke, and piss. It's the only thing she can do, this changing, this channeling, a reserve of divinity. It's her way to Golo and the culmination of her shamanistic studies—secret studies of black sorcery. It was the one spell she had kept hidden from Golo; her ability to shift. Become Ancient.

Thus, it begins.

The hair on her arms thickens, fingers extending, hardening to wooden flesh-sticks, branches without veins, sharp and darkly wet. Her face twists, skin stretches across bone, fattens to the face of something not human, an animal. Her body seizures. She screams to Kala, who does not hear her, and thrashes about the room. She is turning wolf, turning bear and witch and hawk. And as her prayer intensifies, her voice distorts to a sustained growl, something warped and uneven. She snarls, fangs yellowed, tongue distended out of her mouth. And she roars and her roar shatters bottles of entrails. Dead snakes. Pickled hog skin. Skunk eyeballs exploding, slipping off shelves, melting in sticky plops.

It is almost complete.

The frenzy surrounds, becomes her.

The back door to the shed is shadowed in her awful presence. Misao's bones crack out into the night. More bones jut from her back and sides, her legs like she is becoming spider. Her hair frazzles from her head and more hair has sprouted on her cheeks and arms. She throws off her robe, tears it from her body, a phantasmagoric sorceress of the night. Her eyes burn green, black, opal doom. She has become her own Death Head Beast, the incarnation of ancient anti-animism.

Her arms droop, drag across the snow, those wooden fingers digging into the frozen ground. She chugs her way up the hill to where Reich levitates at chest level, his arms outspread, his body spinning. Her inhuman eyes follow the electric corridor that stretches down from the sky as it encircles his body like a three-dimensional shield.

From beyond, animals cry as if something is coming.

Misao gags, spins around, sniffing the air with her deformed snout. She cries out a shrill jag of noise.

Reich's orgone corridor to the sky roars as if pumping him full of orgone. She lurches toward where he lies, his body still spinning, spinning slower now, whooping like helicopter blades. She looks up at the falling snow, how it radiates off the orgone corridor, recalls the blood-spattered accumulator, the vision she suffered, inhales, drawing in the sounds of the animals. And she lets out a terrifying roar that blasts its way across the mesa, that stirs the ground to shiver, stirs earth to shocking life.

She stands before the spinning Reich, enveloped in his orgonotic glow. His head has shrunken, turned a striking white and his mouth hangs open, consumed by static. His nose has receded back into his head. His hair haloes around his head like a crown of white strings.

In one sudden blow, Misao raises her distended arm and strikes down through the orgone and into the vortex of his chest.

His eyes pop from his latex face, static rumble peaking.

Somewhere deep, stretching miles below the earth, drenched in mountains of skull-chopped ice, a humungous dead octopus eye twitches.

Awakens.

Never one to be satisfied, even among the New Golden Dawn's hedonistic desert ceremonies of old, Ukko runs a bony hand over his skinless head and presses one final button.

A high pitched whine.

A wheeze.

Ukko turns to the table, spits a quick, "Shit," from his mouth.

Dorje is not there.

No longer on the operating table.

From behind the table, something coughs over the crackle. Even now, the electricity blips, circuits shooting madly into the air from the wrist and ankle clamps. Whatever is in the corner, through its coughing and gagging, still has electrodes strapped to its head. Wires stretched to break from the console, across the table to what lurks in those shadows.

"Dorje," Ukko says. "Dorje, come to the table. We must continue the procedure in the correct way. This is not the correct way. You must be strapped in like a good boy. You know that. Come now, come."

But Dorje does not come and it is hard to see him from where Ukko stands. Slowly, Ukko moves out from behind the console and, back hugging the wall, cranes his head to see Dorje, to coerce him from a distance back to the table.

The man known as Dorje is no longer Dorje.

Instead, Ukko's eyes bulge, nostrils flare in disgust at the creature before him. Something must have gone wrong, must still be going wrong, for the thing's head pulses a bright orange where the electrodes—now fully sunken into Dorje's head—hum and pulse power.

And Dorje struggles to stand.

Ukko staggers back, arm steadily searching for his chain, for one of his old machine guns, even for Dorje's axe. In all of his years of tapping, he has never seen such a sight.

The restaurant shakes. A tremor.

Something undone.

Something ancient under the ground.

A stirring.

And in that moment, Ukko lunges for Dorje's axe, the closet weapon to him. Dorje has risen, risen to his full height.

And he's terrifying.

Whatever happened to Dorje in the moment of the tapping has completely obliterated his human body. Instead of the handsome young man who entered his laboratory, Ukko cringes at the sight of a hulking mass of fleshy black tar. The thing's eyes are tiny red beads and the mouth too big for the head. Two small nostril holes flare, but Dorje's aching in place as he rises, bones cracking, dripping, bulbous and gross.

Dorje cocks his head, black tar-slime oozing out of his mouth.

Ukko quickly handles the axe, swings it back, and rushes out from behind the console to the table, over the wire pile with the full intention of slamming the axe into Dorje's head, a head still plugged into the system. But there is a quickness in Dorje that Ukko was not expecting, something foreign and fierce. The beast rages forward, knocking over the stretcher where he lied, and head-on into Ukko, throwing them both back to the console.

Wires rip.

Something cracks.

The axe skids from Ukko's grip.

Dorje straddles him, still human underneath the goop that spills over Ukko's skinless face. And through the screams and the howls for it all to stop, Dorje rams his slimed fist into Ukko's face over and over, leaving Ukko nothing but a twitching shit-sack of spaghetti brains and blood.

Dorje stands, limps over to his axe and picks it up. He steps away from the body, but his head is still connected to the wires. He slips on a blood pool, goes down to one knee, back against the overturned operating table.

Something cracks again, behind him. It's the electric current from Ukko's Igniter.

Dorje touches the wrist strap where the current is circling.

The current: blue, sparkling blue.

The extreme blue sensation startles him, but he embraces it and something like a monstrous laugh roars inside him. He opens his mouth and shoves the strap fueled by the current of the Igniter inside. And he stands in the bloody green laboratory, axe at his feet. He shuts his eyes, feels something he's never felt before, a feeling that drains him of the memory of why or who or how he was. It is only him now in this form and the lust for violence that spikes itself through his chest.

He is Kaiju.

His vision ripples with the image of dragons, reptiles, sea creatures roaming the Earth. Powerful land beasts snarling.

A Japanese soldier slicing the neck of a begging peasant. A

skyscraper. The smell of fire and blood drops. Ice cracking for miles. Brains guzzled in the jungle. The scent of a lover. An explosion. A bleating lamb.

A severed paw.

It's as if the entire world cracks open in that moment. It sends him laughing and he bends, picks up the table where he lied and sets it upright.

Black gloves reaching through the dark. A trigger clenched.

Shape in the dark.

White light in the corner of a dark room.

He lies down on the operating table and extends his goopy arms out. His thick legs dangle over the side.

Submersion in water.

Birth under moonlight screams.

Dorje reconnects, shudders.

A gigantic maiden of ice.

Fingers upon fingers.

Murky bog.

In the laboratory, the ground below shakes once again, spilling, clanging, clanging the entire room.

The ceiling cracks. Dorje opens his eyes, watches the dust float waves across the room. He can see every speck and how the specks join with other specks.

Together they go.

But he's slipping into numbness. Something hot from around his temples as if his brain were enlarging, expanding to meet the universe.

To become the universe.

And he raises his hand. His human hand. Skin of a man. A clean, unbrutalized hand. In that moment, there is no laboratory. There is no separation from the churning underfoot to the vast reaches of outer space. But a face hovers above his.

It is not real, wavering.

And his eyes move from human to red and human to red. It is the face of a pale man. Little man. A shrouded-in-blue man.

The face is hate incarnate. And Dorje screams himself to that tar-covered state. To be doused in hate.

To become hate.

It doesn't work. He remains human.

And there's a knock at the doorway, the door already open.

He pulls himself back from the table, looks up.

It's her again, can't be her again. She was just here. He remembers her here. The lifelike image of Ami as she walked across the room and bent close to Golo, Golo sitting at the table in this vignette of a room.

All around the black curtains.

The black fold-like mountains encroaching.

Dark matter.

A vacuum.

A nightmare Dorje doesn't remember entering, only him and the beast within he cannot conjure to be.

Dorje strikes again at Golo. Again his hand blasts through the image. The semblance of a shaman. This is not a real man. Never was a real man.

Door opening, already opened. Ami stands at the door. She's beautiful. The woman he murdered. And she floats across the room in crackles. A starlet. But Golo is gone. Dorje panics, can't breathe, must breathe. He forces a deep breath, chest tightens. The image of the man he wants to kill. And he's gone. But the door opens again. And Ami is beautiful in the doorway. Perhaps, he thinks, this is all there is, this coming and going, this loop upon loop until death and beyond death. Or this is death. And death is all there is. But it can't be this easy. And where is his axe? How did he come here to this space?

Suddenly, Dorje turns and runs to the blackness, but he runs in place. The darkness is a pillow constricting. A jelly one cannot sink into. One that one presses into without moving forward. So he turns, trapped, being trapped inside this thick black skin.

But now, there is a man before him. A man sitting *seiza* style on the table. A man with his eyes crusted shut. And trembling. That man is Golo.

Golo's eyes shoot open. He stands, but not on the table, hovers just inches above the table. Those suspenders. The same *hakama* and overcoat. He opens his hand and blue smoke trails up, up into the blackness, until it becomes the blackness.

Both men watch it go.

Dorje, frozen, hateful, confused and weary, waits for Golo to notice him.

And the door opens. Ami walks into the room, disappears.

The image repeats.

Golo drifts down to the ground and takes in the blackness much like how Dorje did. Dorje steps from the darkness and the stage is two bodies. Two men. And the image of Ami looping in the Void.

"What is this place?" Golo says.

"You're here to kill me," Dorje says.

"I must have—a ritual space, I cannot be sure."

"The death of your wife."

But Golo cannot hear Dorje. Not yet. So Dorje steps to where the light hits the vignette stage, and speaks a mantra, though now, in this sacred space, this Other space, with Golo present, he cannot hear his own prayers. As he mutters the prayers on the periphery, Golo suddenly realizes the immensity of this space, of this scene. The image of his wife fades into his perception. And he understands.

He understands death. As it happened.

As it must happen. For eternity in the conjoining of these minds.

Her face, so close. She loops back to the door. To the table. And back.

Golo follows her, speaking so quickly even he cannot catch his own words, but they are words of what should have been spoken. A warning of what could have been. Him standing in the doorway. Blocking her with his body. The tears. The shivering and shaking. And Dorje on the edge, yet unseen, a man caught in the throes of his own non-prayers. And to the door. To the table. Back again. Golo statics himself into the hologram, tracing Ami's movements. A man possessed. Perhaps, he thinks, if only he can step into her fully, if only he can inhabit her fully, he can become her so as to inhabit her.

To bring her back to life.

To bring her back to life, before—

Murder.

To stop the blood rushing from her skull.

To become the man who would die so she could live.

And this final revelation pulses a spurt of blue up through this throat. It coats his tongue in lucidity.

Golo turns to face Dorje, his charged gaze breaking the man from his invisibility.

Breaking him so they both exist in this same space.

In the Void of Death.

To enact a performance of mutual death.

"So it was you," Golo says. "The man who murdered my wife—I'll crush your soul."

"For my brothers and sisters in death," Dorje says, voice rising. "You'll be emptiness supreme. For all eternity. I am Dorje, your slayer."

"I'll follow you to Hell."

"This is Hell," Dorje says, but Golo has already begun to attack.

Through the door.

Misao is slammed back from the moment of impact with Reich's stomach, her body splitting into more branches, sap, bloody veins gushing red splatters over the snow.

And Reich's body puffs, keeps spinning, emits a shimmering hum.

Misao's eyes boil. She drops to her knees, trembling at the sight of how the mad scientist's body balloons outward. But something below her, all around her, feels unstable. It's the ground. She snorts out a thick breath, teeth grit. She curls her elongated finger-branches inward to form a sloppy fist for the second blow, for in her mind, she believes in the power of slaughter therapy, in the decimation of magick gone wrong.

But a sharp crack—

A wave beneath the brainy earth roars and miles away she hears a building topple. A grand cloud of death-smoke rising.

Reich's body lunges higher into the air, drops, still hovers almost as high as their shack itself. And his head lobs to the side, tongue extended from his mouth, his face melting from the constant spin. And the ground rumbles again, throws Misao back, to a roll, her monstrous face skidding in the snow. Suddenly, another tremor—more than a tremor, a whip-crack—slaps her body into the air, throws her up and down. She roars, cries out, her memory of Golo erupting in her mind, a phantom. She bites into snow, rolls to a creaking stand.

It has already begun.

Miles below the snow—a stirring. A fleshy heartbeat from Nothing to Life. A bulbous body twisting, synapses firing, spurting pink goop over desolate tracts of snow-drenched land. A road cracks, bubbles pink. Windows shatter. Cold insides heating to a boil. And the sudden recognition of pain, the pain of a lopped-off head. Stringy ropes of non-thought. And frozen in blackened earth, eight tentacles extending. Trapped. And move. Move yourself to the night air of those pink spurts. Constrict and kick as if the water has hardened. As if you could move a mountain, break a mountain.

Shake.

Curl muscles to solidify the skeletal frame and the crusted skin that hangs over the shape of your body. For it is time.

Misao charges Reich as the land bubbles beneath her. A pink geyser of brain-juice spits from near the shed, but she can't stop. She mustn't stop now. It's for Golo, for the death of the only man she's truly loved. And so she lunges, wobbling, the ground breaking, splintering for the final blow, transfixed on the floating figure. If only she can jump high enough, but that blue light from the sky has thickened like a paste around his body. Her fingers uncurl and she jumps, throws back her arm to kill him.

And Reich's mouth gushes laughter.

Golo's chest tightens. He can't breathe right—a thickness, a roping choke. He forces himself to inhale, to taste the same air as his wife's killer: how the man's nose arcs to the left of his face, the dark lines below his eyes. The tension in how his fingers shiver. And if this is Hell or one of its incarnations, Golo recognizes the choice to not make things right, but to alter this oblivion in his favor.

To harness the ultimate action as if this were all some kind of staged performance. But there is no crowd, no healing, except to heal the man who stands before him of his life, to take a life that has taken a life. He pushes out another breath, sucks in twice more, until that breathing steadies him, clears his ears to the silence that surrounds them. And Ami. The semblance of her repetitive motion. Like an actress or a robot programmed to repeat. To move from the doorway to the table. Come near and nearer. Be his everything and all.

Breathe.

The satisfaction of wrenching his skin off and smelling just how rotten his heart really is. And Golo plants his feet on the ground, shuts away Ami, the sound of her near end.

Exhale in stutters.

Clack teeth thrice, body rigid.

Become meat.

Still the oscillation to an—

Executioner of love, love as an ending, as the perfect ending to this neophyte scum's existence. And if this space, this non-place theatre, is just a trick of the imagination, a strange form of ritual enactment that operates as hallucination, then so be it and onward to the culmination, but the image of Ami repeats, repeats from a place that Golo does not recognize. No, this is not a hallucination.

This is destiny unleashed.

Dorje's fingers form devil horns arcing at his sides like the young days, the desert days of no return, but those days are far gone and this place with its obsidian walls that echo nowhere, the looping wife. This vignette needs a director.

A rumble in the distance—a sharp crack from above.

A violent unbecoming.

A violent performance.

And as Golo arcs and spins, butoh-mimes toward Dorje, a wind swirls, a breathy wind—Golo's arms in spin, entrancing, clicking momentum, windmilling fists.

Dorje extends his devil-horned hands and prepares for the storm.

It doesn't come.

The rumble above jitters his head.

He looks up.

And for a moment, there is no Golo, no Ami, just the hum of the inside of his head. A quiet fullness one sinks into. In peace eternal. "I'll never be sorry," Dorje whispers, tastes black hair in the back of his throat.

This is when the world goes silent.

This is when Golo's arm blasts through Dorje's back—skin splitting, orchids of organs disrupted—as Ami moves from the door to the table and bends to Nothing.

"How's that for art?" Golo whispers in Dorje's ear, one arm yanking his head to Golo's lips. "It's for her ghost."

The rumble, but Dorje's knees are weak, shivering. He looks down at Golo's hand extending out of his chest, the warmth of the man's body pressing up against him. His breath and a mantra, a new mantra Dorje has never heard bubbling in his ear. Softer.

Softer.

The world cracking above.

The black melting sky.

A vision of murder, bloody flesh.

Golo's other hand squeezes Dorje's neck, holding him ragdoll and he yanks his other arm out from the man's chest, the completion of his own personal Death-Mess performance piece. An ode to vengeance. The sublimity of fisting for life, a vampiric act of transference to end the life of this wife murderer.

And there, watching Dorje crumble to the floor with a fist-sized hole in his chest, that body leaking innards, he hears a shrill cry, something aquatic and beastly.

Something mollusk.

The hum of pink energy.

He remembers the orgone accumulator, the blip before he disappeared, just a foggy moment before his mind cracked.

Breathe.

And Dorje is sucked dry, face to the floor.

The animal mask faces of his brothers and sisters, the ones inside the giant naked dead girl. Hands digging frozen skin, carving a hole to the inside, to the chamber of their conjuration. And the walk to the girl, the walk through the snow. There was a building in the distance. The smell of piss materializing like a trail of smoke, just visible and Dorje had inhaled. He remembered the area, that part of the mesa, the same part where he had slaughtered the orgone woman. The orgone witch. And the sudden force from that piss-reeked building, a form in the dark from afar.

His heart slows, pumping jagged.

The growl of a beast from beyond.

Something inside him raging and—Ukko's death. The pain of regret. He feels it in his guts, guts beginning to leak outward, spread across the ground, at the feet of his killer. At Golo.

And above them both, the squirming begins.

Eyes blinking at dirt, squealing pain. Suffocation.

And it feels as if the mountains around them, those black curtains, are writhing, stretching outward.

Golo jumps on the table as if doing so would somehow break the trance of his virtual wife, her static visage and the beauty of it all. But she's slowing down now, her body blinking. Fading.

And even though Golo extends his arm toward her, the same arm he used to eviscerate Dorje, blook-cloaked and shaking, he knows she will not come.

But it's the final gesture. An act in and of itself.

His way of saying—

What's coming down from above.

Golo looks up to the blackness, just in time to see the splatter of pink brain descending like a tidal wave.

His fingers go stiff.

And he screams.

Tables break. A chair hurled through an already shattered window. Two creeps in jean jackets, bandanas and war paint, wielding uzi machine guns storm the dilapidated restaurant, cackling, spraying the place with bullets. A door kicked off its hinges. A green-lit room blood-painted, rotten stench. Like fish.

A growl, a gurgle from the shadows.

Claws skitter.

"Clean done Swiss-Cheesed this son of a bitch," one of the thugs says, surveying the seemingly empty establishment.

A plate breaks from near the kitchen.

"What's that?" the other says.

"Probably a damn stink running up the place—or my next meal, more like."

"Judging by the green room back there, I'd say someone already beat you to—" but a fiery shot of pain halts his words, chokes the end of the sentence from his tongue. And he looks out and down, his body fish-flopping on the floor, separated at the waist.

His friend jumps back, was just a whirl of blackness, a stench that cut between them and now crashing back into the kitchen. "The shit?!"

But the halved guy is too much of a squealer, bloody mouth gurgling death. His friend shoots him once in the face, mashing his visage to mush. "Sorry . . . " he says, panting, already spinning behind him to whatever thing in the kitchen rushed in and did this. He crouches, his Uzi pointed toward a fresh clatter of woks and oil bottles, cans crashing to the ground. "Better come out now," he yells, "cause I'm coming in."

But he's not.

And he doesn't.

It's hard to charge when you're gripped by the neck, lifted off the ground. All you can do is piss, and he pisses right down his jeaned leg, over his sneakers. His Uzi clatters to the ground, stomped by whatever abomination holds him airless in the dark. Through the bloody light of that green room behind him, he sees the wretched face in front of him, blurring harder by the second as the beast squeezes, claws breaking skin like choking a banana. And this nameless thug of the desolate city grinds his teeth, stares into the face of the abyss and dies throatless.

He dies moments before the first building in the city topples from the rough rumble of the mollusk monster who causes the streets to crack and the sounds of the dead screaming, the near dead, the heroin addicts, meth punks, speed freaks, rapists, murderers, and all denizens of this worldly hell, shaken to life in the dark by the sudden eruption.

The earth's yawn.

Blood and snow.

And it's quick—

Quick death, explosions of timber and concrete, steel and glass embedded in eyeballs, exploding faces, needles snapping off in arms. The slow drift of a junkie's death. Of a metal band electrocuted on stage in front of their audience of epileptic zombies, the narcoleptic lunatics who stalk the city. The city on fire. The city a scream of swirling death.

Of mollusk scent.

Of eight tentacles shooting up out of the ground—one rising in the middle of the mesa, one in the city center, and others up through houses and brothels, crashing roads and men, women screaming for a life they never knew, crushed by the slime and dirt-drenched suction cups, those writhing arms of the sea beast who rises.

Who lives.

Who gasps air and squeals eardrums to burst.

But across town at that dilapidated restaurant, a monstrous Dorje, now a hairy creature of snarling violence, stands still holding the throat of the dead thug in his hands and squeezes, keeps squeezes even as the walls of the restaurant crumble and crack around him.

He bolts outside, the roof exploding in a fury of steel, wood, and wires. The crackle of electricity. The stench of dead fish. Grains of burnt rice.

And beyond the monstrous Dorje witnesses the leviathan's wrath through his inhuman eyes and nose, the taste of rust on his tongue, of blood. A thick tentacle flailing, having crashed up through the bloody concrete, twists and smashes into a glass building, thundering down onto the street, smothering a gang of gutterpunks, squashing the scrambling denizens. One holding on, just a speck from Dorje's beastly view, and the speck is flung, flies off into the night, the scream fading, quieter—

To the night sky shivering under fur.

And a blue beam of light, a tunnel of light in the distance from the place where the beast is drawn. He sees it, breath gravelly and jagged. And he roars gorilla and pig, a braying horse, a bleating sheep. A swell of muscle and fur.

The blue light of his other self—the way.

He lurches off into the snow. The tentacle behind him still raging. The sound of more screaming, jeeps exploding, tires squealing, and another tentacle blasting out through the city, gunshots blaring, heralding—

The beginning of a resurrection.

Across the snow, to the north, near the zones of unpredictability, a giant naked girl lies frozen in the snow, a wound under her breast steaming blood vapor, a wound suddenly trembling and moving as if the edges of the hole were tiny tendrils. And those tendrils writhe toward each other, skin forming to skin.

And the girl's fingers curl, a gush of breath surging out from her lungs. She coughs blood, spits bones and smoke from her mouth, terrified.

And alone.

The ground waves beneath her, the snow a sheet from which she casts off and struggles to rise.

The back of her head, the black draining her hair to a yellow sheen, is blood-stained and smashed, but the squirm of so many tendrils sew furiously to heal her wound to health.

Silently, she stands.

A gorgeous giant in the cold among the calling of the wolves and the caribou, the whistling wind and snow.

She sees a tentacle smashing up the city beyond, but it's too far and she hasn't been to the city in years. Or a time out of time.

The death inside her.

The blue light in the distance. She knows that light. A warmth spreads through her body and she takes her first step, the ground shaking around her.

Even from here, she feels the orgone.

Her calling.

As if it were coming from her home, her once upon a time home.

Misao's mutated hand strikes hard, blows her back yet again. Reich's laughter, a staccato chuckling dread, but the ground won't stop convulsing and wind sears across the mesa. A gust. A tearing of fabric, amplified voltage. Reich's body like a sick bubble expanding. And Misao roars, her weird hands cupping, scratching against her animal ears. She lurches to the shed, to her Golo's remains in the orgone accumulator.

She breaks down the door to the shed, disoriented by how its tiny size has expanded to that of a giant warehouse like the torture halls of her island home. But inside the shed, a force pushes against her body, a heaviness. It's coming from the accumulator. The pressure of water or air. A heady constriction. Misao cannot speak, couldn't speak even if she wanted to, her tongue a jagged tangle of skin and bark. Arm outstretched, she staggers to the accumulator door, to its bloody window with the sloppy stains of Golo's blood.

But that force swells. She inhales, shrieks out a cry, her nerves fluttering.

She steps closer, the force rising.

And the closer she gets, the louder she hears Reich's terrible cackle, becomes more and more aware of her own heart pumping—the blow of an axe to the back of a head, a tumble to the floor—and the blood on the window evaporates to neon blue and smoke seeping from the cracks in the accumulator door. She pushes past the pain, her appendages screaming, cracking, sap spitting out behind her.

To touch the door.

To regain Golo's life and maybe there is a way she can salvage the blood like how Golo salvaged the vomit from his last performance. Even if it means casting the shaman in a new form, so be it and let it become. She's crying, each movement is a mountain and the entire shed shifts to the left, to the right. An imminent collapse.

She touches the door.

The orgone accumulator sucks her arm to its blue heat. And she can neither press nor pull herself away and now, , it's only a second before the orgone consumes her, sucks her flesh to whatever horrific end Golo must have met. She struggles to force herself in, to pry open the door and explode. Anything to meld herself to whatever reality Golo has died into.

The door explodes outward and Misao loses consciousness like the crack of a whipping stick.

Gone she goes, sliding across the floor, tumbling out into the night.

And the orgone accumulator door bursts, breaks, destroyed from its mollusk-brained hinges, releasing a flow of orgone energy out into the night.

The night a bright blue.

A wall of orgone.

The release is final.

The blue is sucked into the lungs of a giant naked stranger who stalks the outer edge, making her way to the blurry mass of Wilhelm Reich, Misao, and the orgone accumulator.

A pale face looming over the hill that borders Golo's shack. Misao sprouts hairy branches from her ribs, feels the branches drip, pulled to the ground, to the tremoring brain-snow beneath. And unless her vision has dimmed, shifted, she sees the snow as a dull pink as if the octopus brain is flooding, turning liquid or hotter, melting the snow. But a tentacle from the other hill fingers up into the air and crashes down. Reich's body lunges upward, drops back to its hovering position, still caught in the blue orgone funnel of light.

And the pale face over the hill is Ami.

Misao has seen her pictures in the spellbooks and texts Golo keeps boxed in the closet of his shack's sleeping room. The top of her head is stained black at the roots, but it's her. And she's gigantic. Misao tries to speak, tries once more to reach out a hand, but she can't move. The branches from her body have driven themselves into the ground and already she feels the pink swelling through the core and soon it will reach her body. Misao does not know the effects, but such a dose directly to the bloodstream is surely fatal.

Ami is transfixed by the spinning Reich. A smile breaks on her face, but she cocks her head to the side, her body stiffening with each step, curious. The hole in her chest is a loosely-skinned patch. It glows red and at the right angle her heart beats smoky and pounds her body to step across the shaking ground. The tentacle whips out less than a mile away, writhing its power, slams down hard enough to elevate Ami off the ground for just a second. The shed cracks. The blue light intensifies.

But another stands puppeted near the shed, the shed aflame with blue orgone energy. And Ami has never felt anything like it in her life. Or death. And now this creature, a presence Ami feels. She feels the creature's closeness to Golo as if the creature were the cause of her death and the orgone fills Ami with the death of Golo, with his disappearance, fueling her feet, up to her cranium vertex with the lust to end this creature's life. To meld this monster to her heart if it could only soothe the regret and confusion she feels.

But something from inside the shed breaks. Ami hears the sound and she's at the door, moving to the table, to look over the plans for the accumulator before the world goes red. Then black. And frozen.

No—this is something else.

A growling wolf-like abomination storms from the shed, shields its eyes from the orgone light and the spinning Reich, from the blast of orgone emanating from the shed, splitting up into the sky. And at that moment, Ami looks dead into the heart of her own killer—Dorje.

Dorje senses nothing but bloodlust. Whoever he was, he is not.

He will conquer orgone.

Misao tries wrenching herself from the ground, for whatever evil mess of an animal that has found its way inside Golo's shack snarls with blood-fever. She shuts her eyes and lets the weight of the branches go where they will. She lets them sink, feels the weight of her pushing cease.

Behind her, the warmth of the shed's orgone energy hits her back and the pink brain of the mollusk fills her mouth. She's underground at another black box venue in the city's southern quadrant. It's dusk and Golo contorts himself on stage, the head of a latex rooster looking out at the crowd, at the sick and the unwanted. She holds a honey-coated rebar she pounds on the floor and prays to Kala. A circular prayer, thick and loud. Golo throws himself on the ground, his complimentary squawks forming the prayer's inverse. She feels her head grow hot with nectar, the drip of their mutual meditation. Of their synergy. And suddenly, the venue turns orange light and heat. She thrusts the rebar harder into the ground, cracking the stage as Golo thunders himself in the head, screaming the prayer, until his voice turns rock and wind. This, thinks Misao, is what she needs. That moment of all moments. The connection, a connection even beyond death. There is no death. There is only the continuation of forms. Shells. So she sinks. With the wicked creature charging from the shack to where she stands rooted, she sinks. She cannot fight. A paroxysm of unbecoming. Of wanting to splatter this gory creature in his—

Ami quickly turns to catch Dorje running over the cracked earth to the rooted creature, the creature who feels to Ami like woman and hate, jealousy and a thousand deaths. She sucks the orgone deep inside her, though, and watches the little Reich turn into nothing but a fleshy mass of blue skin churning. So she does what she did when she was alive and smaller. When she, the orgonotic shaman would turn crowds to drooling masses of bliss. She cups her hands and feels the orgone solidify. She draws a breath—two, three, four—for the sky and beyond the universe, overcome with the truth of orgone.

But she fails to see the tentacle that's snaked its way across the dirt and how the ground is now a bright pink, a pink that seeps into her dead skin, coats the bottom of her feet with a weird numbing hate. The tentacle wraps around her neck and yanks her off her feet.

Dorje lunges toward the hateful creature before him, but mid-air, he catches sight of a mountainous tentacle choking around the neck of the giant naked girl who pulses blue. And the tentacle whips the girl into the air and slams her to the ground.

The shed explodes, sending planks of wood barreling into

Dorje's body. The wood nails the rooted creature, but where is the rooted creature? Dorje is knocked back, pummeled and confused.

And the sound of a woman screaming with lungs the size of the ocean, tearing apart the tentacle that held her tight. Yes, Ami's snapped off the tentacle and throws it toward the flaming city beyond. She watches the bloody chunk of tentacle rooted to the beast who writhes under her flail and gush a thick purple out its wound. But the shed has exploded in a tornado of blue orgone energy.

But that only does not cause her jaw to open, to hang in hollow wonder.

No, the root of her confusion is the man who stands in the middle of the rubble, enveloped in thick smoke and blue light. A man she knows and loves.

Golo.

All of a sudden, though, the orgone and the mollusk brain coating her feet conjoin within the dead-live Ami, paralyzing her to the seeping shaking ground in a storm of electricity.

The last thing Golo recalls is standing over a gored Dorje—the man who slaughtered his wife. In an obsidian blankness. A vignette from elsewhere. And all that came after. The gloves. The static blare from his mouth to the perineum. An arc. A spreading of skin. He dissolved and the tiny speck of who he thought he was cast to the abyss. To a blue sea of flat lines. He became a thinness. Then a line. Then a split edge and out into the fiery spool of an explosion on unsound ground. The quaking and the pink snow. A wind on his eyeballs. Inhale and back. Be present in mist. He steps from the smoke, steps over steel and metal, wooden planks, looks up to see—

She's there.

His Ami.

She casts away a chunk of mollusk and the naked sublime, his heart races to his cranium, a wet pulse. The nectar stiffens his back like a broomstick. "We've found the way," he says to himself, but here, there is no Misao. And the blue light from the sky, a light pushing around a ball of flesh emits a trill, a hard pulse, both thick and wet. The tears gush. He grits his teeth, shoves away the pain in his jaw. He steps further over planks and rubble, over shattered tools, racing toward his wife if only for her to hold him close to her heart like it always should have been. Never was.

A mutated hand, more claw than hand, reaches up from the rubble and grabs Golo by the ankle, forcing him down. He topples, his head cracking into a board, spraying his eyes with blood. And the monster rises from the pile, a bloody heap of fur and bubbling skin. The stench of rot. Of shit. Golo tries to move, but a clawed fist slams into his face, angling his vision to his wife in the throes of electrocution. He screams, kicks at the monster, but the beast is upon him. He throws his hands to the thing's face, trying to keep himself from being consumed and the creature's mouth opens, revealing row upon row of jagged teeth and that smell. He's smelled it before. It's the smell of his wife's killer. A pungent smell like being inside a body. The waft of men and women in animal masks and the heat of a grope, of claws and fangs. He pushes against the inhuman creature, but he's weak. And this is it.

Hot teeth sink to ragged skin.

A quietude beyond the pain. But the heat on Golo's skin is not the heat of a death-bite. It is something below him, something earthy encompassing him, twining around his limbs and moving him through the rubble. A hot pink sea to rest in, to be carried away from the snapping of jaws. And snarls.

He touches the root swirling around his body, a coating of skin around his face and the movement through the pink sludge, the quivering ground. He hears destruction, a grinding gloom, but it's far away and the screams melt to the hum of his own head as the roots coat over his ears.

Golo is lifted through the rubble by arms of wooden skin, turned pink. And hot. The hotness wakes him, lifts him and sends him into the electric arms of his wife. Of Ami.

And she holds him to her breast. Golo opens his mouth to suck the brain out from inside her body. To take all the pain and swallow it forevermore. He sucks harder at the air, those arms holding him, rocking him as if he's climbed the tallest tree in the forest, and Ami's face is so close. He feels her breath on his face, inhales and keeps drawing his breath to swallow the pink from her body. To let her know he's sorry for her death and the pain in not being able to give her his own life. For the chance to look his love in the eye and for a moment, all is well in the world. The screams. The quaking ground of death. The orgone storm. And Ami smiles into his eyes, into the tips of his toes. A radiance. The ultimate shamanic act.

Of love.

"Thank you," Golo says.

"Good night," Ami says. "Good night once more."

But below, Dorje slashes at a struggling Misao. He severs a root, her blood spitting across the pink brain landscape. Enraged, he claws and bites at her spidery fur, at her wooden skin and the branches that hold Golo up to his lover. The animal Dorje wants nothing but to kill, to destroy this other feeling he gets from the performance happening around him. But with each slash and cut, any power that the orgone might have given him, fades. And Misao screams with each cut, but holds Golo, holds him tight in her arms.

"And goodbye," Ami says, suddenly twisting away from Golo and scooping up the raging beast of Dorje. She holds him in her hand as a mighty gorilla might hold a dandelion. And she brings him close to her face, her non-live mind stripping away the beast within him, knowing his true self—the murderer. And if only she had an axe. If only she had the strength and prowess to strike his skull and split him in two. She looks back at Golo, still hovering before her, lets him see the beast she holds in her hand.

Golo nods. And they both know.

In one quick motion, Ami plucks the beast's head from his neck like slaughtering a chicken. Such a puny action, a simple gesture. The plucking of a flower. A stroke and a fizzle of blood. The release of the beast's bowels and she squeezes her hand, feels his waste mush to his skin and fur. She opens and squeezes yet again, balling the beast into nothing more than trash. To make him go away. To grind him to dust. And his mushy head hits the ground. Misao's unrooted foot rises and stomps on his head like pounding that rebar on the stage. She hears bone mash. It's harder than stomping fruit, but the stomp is a release and the pink brain sucks his blood into its fold.

And stills.

The world. The mollusk. A sudden breath of Nothing.

Then Ami reaches down once more, her breath warm on Golo's face and he's swallowed the pink that consumed her, has become stuffed with whatever pain she had suffered. He doesn't care. No death. And even so. It no longer matters how much pain he feels and he's learned this. He would give anything to her. Anything to just know he could hold her, but she's breaking up once again as if the show has come to an end. Now, she crackles static, little bits of her body floating up off her body as if her skin were peeling away.

From inside her chest Golo hears the ping of a temple bell, but it's a pleasant ping, something that melts his stomach to flutter.

Suddenly, Ami reaches for Golo, uncurls him from Misao's loving grip, sets him away from the rubble, near the shack and its inner glow.

Feet touching the ground, Golo fails to notice that the snow has stopped falling, the ground is not shaking. And he pulls his overcoat over his chest, to the crackle of the inferno in the distance. "Let it burn," he says. "To ashes goes the past."

But he stares in wonder at the sight of Ami as she gently plucks Misao's mutated form from the ground, those roots sliding out easy and she lifts Misao, places her to the place where her skin has coated over the wound. And with her gaze on Golo, she purses her lips and inserts Misao into her heart.

The act seems to pain Ami, for her body shakes, her skin still petaling up into the night air. And near her, the bubble of Reich rises, rises higher into the sky, until he turns into a speck, and gone.

"No," Golo says. "Don't go—please."

But he knows she must. He drops to his knees, arms limp at his sides and watches as Ami's body turns from the blue of orgone energy to a bright sheet and, shaking, she raises her arms, looks down once more at Golo and vanishes in a glaring cloud of neon.

A becoming. A farewell, until the light is too bright for him to watch.

He throws his hands over his eyes to quell the tears. To finally feel closure, to let the flutters spew pink from his mouth. And he breathes through his nose, retching out the pain he took from her, watches it seep into snow. Without looking, he reaches up and touches Misao's hand. The touch of her soft skin is a reverberation within him, a homecoming.

"She did it for you," Misao whispers.

And Golo smiles yellow teeth and stubble, face weary and beaten. Yes, he smiles.

For Ami.

For the breaking dusk smearing the sky purple and red splatters. Of a brief moment of purification.

It's what he'd been waiting for.

It's a wish he dared never speak.

But it's time for sleep. A bed for two. And two hearts breathing heart to pumping heart—for the coming of nectar.

The carnival draws hundreds; those left from the mollusk-quake, those left to rebuild from the ashes of the dead city.

In a brightly-lit black box theatre, a man places a tub of bluish skin petals in the center of the stage. A woman holds the severed tail of seven rattlesnake tails bound in pink clay. She shakes the tails, turns up the volume on a homemade console strung busy with multi-colored wires. A current snapping every six seconds. Another level adjustment cues a deeper tone. An oscillation. A high-pitched squeal. And the man on the stage is not smeared in pink brain. A contact microphone has been affixed to the top of his jaw. It shoots warm pulses of energy to his cranium, to amplify the nectar drip. And a drum, the field recording of an ancient drum slips, surrounds the crowd from the speakers hanging from the ceiling. An omniscope of aural healing. The man's eyes are coated blue. A throaty breath unfolding, crisp and consuming. The woman shakes her head to the rhythm, to the warmth of the crowd's energy as it converges in a visible aura of orgonotic nectar. An ode on how to go on. How to begin and let go.

Golo looks back at Misao and nods.

For there is another level to their performance, a significance of static, the static Misao blends from yet another channel on the mixing board. It is the final piece. A way to reach into the hearts of those who have gathered to participate in the event.

And it begins.

When Golo draws the energy into his lungs, deeper to a place of liquid forgetting, he holds it there and rises, stands tall above the crowd as a man who has breached the Void and lived to turn it into cathartic therapy.

Misao stomps once on the ground, screams her adoration at Golo.

Golo opens his mouth, releases the energy, and vomits orgone all over the crowd, an action of love, clear to the cranium, like swinging an axe into the trunk of a living tree.

ABOUT THE AUTHOR

Jamie Grefe writes within rooms of the darkly comedic, the surreal, and the horrific. His first book, *The Mondo Vixen Massacre*, was published in 2013 by Eraserhead Press. In 2015, Rooster Republic Press published his surrealistic love letter to Japan, *Domo ArigaDIE!!!* Grefe is also responsible for the official novelizations of comedians Tim Heidecker and Gregg Turkington's Adult Swim webseries *Decker: Classified* and *Decker: Port of Cal l: Hawaii*. His short work has appeared in *Birkensnake, elimae, LIES/ISLE, New Dead Families* and *Sein Und Werden* among other places. *Unfinished Business*, a feature length horror film he cowrote, is currently in postproduction. Grefe has also worked with performance artist Rudolf Eber (of Runzelstirn and Gurgelstock) as well as film director and producer Jim Wynorski. Grefe's website is http://jamiegrefe.com

Boiled Americans by Michael Allen Rose

Boiled Americans is a puzzle box in book form, inspired by the violence of living in urban America and exploding the tendency to forget or ignore.

Great American Slasher by David C. Hayes

Baseball, apple pie . . . and murder.

The Bohemian Guide to Monogamy
by Andrew Armacost

Here, a strange labyrinth of interlinked short fiction assembles itself into a darkly moving novella that deftly explores the bottomless pain and pleasure of love and commitment, the hinterland between youth and adulthood.

Surreal Worlds edited by Sean Leonard

An anthology of surrealistic compositions created by some of the finest names in genre fiction. A showcase of international talent undaunted by the conventions of language and common narrative structures. Here is timelessness. Here is Surreal Worlds

How to Succesfully Kidnap Strangers by Max Booth III

Do not respond to bad reviews. If you must respond to bad reviews, please do not kidnap the reviewer.

ADHD Vampire by Matthew Vaughn

He came, he conquered, he was distracted a lot

Notes from the Guts of a Hippo
by Grant Wamack

A rugged journalist travels to Brazil in search of a missing hippo researcher and the notes left behind lead to something earth shatteringly revelatory.

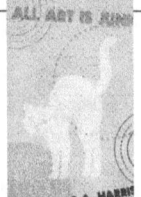

All Art is Junk by R. A. Harris

Lana Rivers, a girl with paintbrush hair, is missing and it's up to Lancelot, her cyborg knight, and his bionic conjoined twin, Cilia, to find her before her evil father, a disrespected artist turned mad-scientist, performs a terrible experiment on her.

Cherub by David C. Hayes

Cherub wasn't like the other boys—too slow, too rough—but he didn't deserve what that hospital did to him, and now he will make them pay.

Skinners by Adam Millard

Los Angeles, the City of Angels. At least, that's what the brochure says. What it fails to mention is the earthquakes. Oh, and the flesh-eating creatures lying dormant beneath the concrete, waiting for the chance to surface once again. Their wait is over . . .

The After-Life Story of Pork Knuckles Malone by MP Johnson

What's a farm boy to do when his pet pig becomes an evil, decaying hunk of ham with slime-spewing psychic powers?

A Lightbulb's Lament by Grant Wamack

A gentleman with a lightbulb for head wakes up in a world full of darkness, hooks up with a beautiful ex-prostitute, and an old man who can heal people; he travels down south to find the mysterious Creator.

The Horror Show by Vincenzo Bilof

A poetry novel—a narcoleptic, amnesiac Nobel Prize-winning poet becomes the subject of an experiment to cure madness.

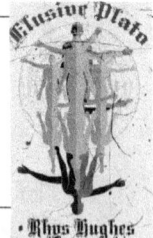

Elusive Plato by Rhys Hughes

The last in a long decadent line of piratical Spanish eccentrics, Bartleby Cadiz grows up in isolation to be as mad, bad and metaphysical as his ancestors. But he feels there is something different about him. What can it be?

Gravity Comics Massacre
by Vincenzo Bilof

An absolutely shitty novella involving comic books, aliens, a serial killer, teenagers in an abandoned town, horror-trope dream sequences, and an ending you're going to hate.

Glue by Scott Lange

Sticky bowels and sticky situations.

Ascent by Matthew Bialer

Is the 8 foot tall creature haunting a small town in Iowa in the fall of the year 1903 the product of a hoax and collective imagination or was it one of the first documented paranormal event in America? This epic poem grapples with these questions.

Fecal Terror by David Bernstein

A killer turd is on the loose!

The Fairy Princess of Trains
by Christopher Boyle

Danny's mediocre life turns upside-down when his couch starts whispering to him. Then he's charged with a supernatural mission: Rescue the Fairy Princess of Trains.

Terence, Mephisto & Viscera Eyes
by Chris Kelso

9 new science fiction stories from Chris Kelso

Industrial Carpet Drag by Bruce Taylor

Chemicals make you do great things!

Bizarro Bizarro: An Anthology

The finest bizarro short stories from 2013.

Necrosaurus Rex by Nicolas Day

Necrosaurus Rex tells the tale of Martin, a simple janitor, who takes an unfortunate trip through time, becomes a violent mutant, and the father of us all. There's 14 billion years crushed inside these pages, and most of them are pretty nasty.

Day of the Milkman by S. T. Cartledge

In a world dominated by the milk industry, only one milkman survives after a terrible storm sinks all the ships and throws the Great White Sea out of balance.

Moosejaw Frontier by Chris Kelso

An unapologetic disaster of metafiction

The Boy Who Loved Death by Hal Duncan

From blackest humour to bleakest horror, with twisted relish, Hal Duncan's eighteen tales dig into death—and the life that goes with it.

X's for Eyes by Laird Barron

Between the machinations of the disciples of black gods and good old corporate skullduggery, it's winding up to be of a hell of a summer vacation for the Tooms Brothers.

Omega Grey by Seb Doubinsky

When professor Todd Bailer embarked on a psychedelics quest to discover if the land of the Dead really existed, he had no idea he would threaten the cosmic balance of the universe by triggering a real-estate conquest of the new Frontier.

Berzerkoids by MP Johnson

The first short story collection from Wonderland Book Award-winning author MP Johnson

Retch by David Bernstein

What would you do if you were cursed to puke right before you reached orgasm? You'd do anything, right? (You know you would.) Find out what one wealthy, good-looking, playboy will do to try to end his abhorrent curse.

www.ingramcontent.com/pod-product-compliance
Lightning Source LLC
Chambersburg PA
CBHW072030170626
46811CB00008B/3017